Wyatt

TWILIGHT FALLS BOOK FOUR

A.M. SALINGER

COPYRIGHT

Wyatt (Twilight Falls #4)
Copyright © 2020 by A.M. Salinger
All rights reserved. Registered with the US Copyright Office.
Second paperback edition: 2024
ISBN: 978-1-9162270-2-6

www.AMSalinger.com
shop.adstarrling.com

Edited by www.ElfwerksEditing.com
Cover Design by A.M. Salinger

BOOKS BY A.M. SALINGER

Nights

One Night - 1

The Escort - 2

Tokyo Heat - 3

Sweet Obsession - 4

Sweet Possession - 5

The Proposition - 6

Undisclosed - 7

Hush - 8

One Day - 9

Twilight Falls

Alex - 1

Carter - 2

Hunter - 3

Wyatt - 4

Drake - 5

Tristan - 6

Miles - 7

CHAPTER ONE

Two Years Ago.

"Are you sure?"

A faint smile curved Nathan Hardy's lips as he studied the man across the desk from him. He could tell Cain Sawyer was worried about him despite the frown darkening his rugged face.

"Positive."

The lines furrowing Cain's brow deepened. "If you need more time, I'll talk to the other partners and—"

"You don't have to do that, Cain. I've made up my mind."

Cain opened his mouth, paused, and released a rueful sigh.

"You always were a stubborn bastard, even when we were in college," he muttered.

Nathan grinned and climbed to his feet. "And you've been a great boss and friend." A twinge shot down his left thigh. He masked a grimace at the cramp.

Cain rose and escorted him to the elevator. "I'll call you when I've organized a farewell party."

"You don't need to do that," Nathan protested. "I'm the one deserting you guys."

Cain narrowed his eyes. "You're having a party, end of story. I'm not letting the best designer in Seattle leave my firm without a proper goodbye."

Nathan rubbed the back of his neck, conscious of the stares they were attracting. "Alright."

"And don't be a stranger when you're back in town," Cain said. Nathan startled when the other man pulled him in for a quick hug. "There'll always be a job here for you if you change your mind."

Nathan swallowed the sudden lump in his throat.

"Thanks, Cain. I don't know what I've done to deserve a friend like you."

Cain's eyes gleamed. "If you're having regrets—"

"I'm not." Nathan flashed him a remorseful smile. "Not about this."

He rode the elevator to the first floor, exited the high rise, and paused on the sidewalk. Horns honked on the busy avenue in front of him. Nathan ignored the hustle and bustle of the traffic and the crowd milling around him, and turned to gaze at the building he'd just walked out of.

This is it. I'm officially out of a job.

That thought should have scared the living daylights out of him. Except it didn't. Not much did these days.

Well, they do say nearly dying does that to people.

His leg throbbed again, reminding him of the reason why he'd just quit the dream job he'd worked so hard for over the years. Nathan clenched his teeth and massaged his stiff thigh muscles. He hadn't fully stretched this morning after his run. He waited until the spasm passed, raised his face to the hazy blue sky, and took a deep breath.

Today was the start of the rest of his life.

He turned right and headed down the avenue. By the time he'd walked the two miles to his apartment building, his limp had become more evident.

Lisa would kill me if she saw me right now.

The thought of the bubbly and energetic physical therapist brought a smile to Nathan's face as he crossed the lobby. Though he hadn't been the most agreeable patient when they'd first met, Lisa had never given up on him. He knew the reason he could walk and run again was due to her perseverance over the past eight months. His smile faded when he recalled their last appointment the day before.

Who knew she'd cry so much?

A bolt of sadness stabbed through Nathan as he got off the elevator on the tenth floor. Saying goodbye to his old life was proving to be much harder than he'd thought it'd be.

He inserted his key in the door of his condo and paused.

It was already unlocked.

There were only two people beside him who had keys to his apartment. His former fiancée Melissa Klein and his brother Dean.

The smell of camellias greeted him when he entered the condo.

Nathan sighed and made a mental note to berate his brother. Dean had obviously told Melissa he was going into the office to hand in his letter of resignation. She would never have come over if she'd known he'd be there otherwise.

He found her on her knees in the bedroom, with her head buried in the closet. Nathan glanced at the half-stuffed overnight bag on the floor before clearing his throat.

Melissa startled and whirled around. "God!" She pressed a hand to her chest. "You scared the crap out of me!"

The guilt he'd been living with these last few weeks stormed through him all over again when he saw the shadows under her eyes and her pinched lips.

"Sorry."

They stared at each other in silence, unspoken words swirling in the air between them. It was two months to the day since Nathan had broken off their engagement.

Melissa's expression grew guarded. "I didn't know you'd be back so soon. I'll be out of your hair as fast as I can."

She turned and started rooting around the closet again.

Nathan hesitated. "Do you want a coffee?"

Melissa stiffened. "No."

Nathan leaned a shoulder against the doorframe.

He felt tired all of a sudden. "You're not even going to look at me?"

Melissa whipped around, her blonde hair flying around her face and her blue eyes bright with barely suppressed anger.

"What do you want me to look at, Nathan?! You dumped me three weeks before our goddamn wedding!"

Shit.

Nathan clenched his jaw and ran a hand through his hair.

"It was the right thing to do, Mel. I know you don't believe me right now, but I would have made you miserable."

A muscle jumped in Melissa's cheek. "Why? Because you don't think I would have coped with the reality that you might be crippled?" Her knuckles whitened on the sweatshirt she was holding. "I'm not that shallow, Nathan!"

He walked inside the room and sat on the edge of his bed. *Their* bed.

"I know you aren't, Mel. And that's why I needed to let you go. Because—" He faltered.

Melissa's throat worked convulsively. "Because what, Nathan?"

Nathan took a shallow breath.

Here goes.

"Because I think I was in love with the idea of being in love with you. As were you."

Melissa recoiled as if he'd physically slapped her,

the color draining from her face. Nathan fisted his hands in his lap.

God, forgive me for being such an asshole.

There were many things he had come to regret since he'd woken up in the hospital ten months ago, days after the horrific accident that had taken place on Christmas Eve. He'd been heading home to see his family in Bellevue after completing one of the biggest projects of his career when a truck had slipped on an icy patch of road on the opposite side of the highway and careened across the median and into oncoming traffic.

Nathan was one of a handful of people who had survived the multi-vehicle collision that had claimed six lives that day and three more later in the hospital. He was put into a medically induced coma and had three rounds of surgery to fix his ruptured spleen and smashed leg before they woke him up.

It was only when he saw pictures of the accident and the remains of his car that Nathan realized how close to death he'd been. According to his doctors, it was a miracle he wasn't paralyzed from the waist down after his body was almost crushed in half by the dashboard of his Prius.

The months Nathan had spent in the hospital and rehab had made him face some hard truths.

There was more to life than working all the hours God made, however passionate he was about his job.

He wasn't in love with Melissa.

And he desperately needed a change of pace and scenery.

Dean was the first person he'd admitted these new and terrifying feelings to. Although his younger brother had looked like he was ready to punch his lights out for deciding to dump Melissa weeks before their wedding, he'd been by Nathan's side when the latter had finally spoken to their parents about his future plans.

Nathan had known that breaking things off with Mel would hit them hard, since she was the daughter of their closest friends. And he'd been ready for their angry words and recriminations. But he'd misjudged how traumatic nearly losing their firstborn son had been on Ben and Helen Hardy. Though they'd expressed their disappointment, they'd not shunned him.

Melissa, on the other hand, had not been as forgiving.

Nathan knew ending their engagement was the right thing to do. He didn't love her, not the way he should love the person he intended to spend the rest of his life with. He'd realized this when he'd seen her for the first time after the accident. It was as if a veil had been lifted from his eyes and he could see everything clearly for the first time in his life.

"Do you really mean that?"

Melissa's hoarse words brought him back to the present.

Nathan gazed at the woman he had hurt and cursed his old self once more.

"I like you, Mel. A lot. As a friend." His lips stretched in a thin smile. "As a lover. But I don't *love* you the way a husband should love his wife. I know I sound like a callous bastard right now, but trust me when I say that I'm the wrong man for you. You deserve better, Mel. You deserve true love and a happy ever after. You deserve a man who will cherish you for the beautiful person that you are."

Tears bloomed in Melissa's eyes. A sob escaped her throat.

Nathan rose and went to her then. As he knelt on the floor of his bedroom and closed his arms around the woman he had wounded so badly with his words and actions, he made a promise to himself.

He had been given a second chance at a life. He doubted the Heavens would give him a stab at true love too. But if they did, if the person he was truly meant to be with ever crossed his path, he would cling on to them and never let them go. And he would treasure them for the rest of his life.

CHAPTER TWO

EIGHTEEN MONTHS AGO.

I'm never going to fall in love again.

Wyatt Batista twisted his champagne flute between his fingers and looked out over the beautiful gardens stretching out beyond the stone terrace. Gathered under a sumptuous rose pergola a short distance away, the bride and groom's families were having their pictures taken with the happy couple.

Wyatt's heart twisted with an age-old ache as he stared at the face of the man he had secretly been in love with for more years than he'd care to admit.

Brandon Taylor's eyes shone with adoration as he gazed at his bride. It was obvious to everyone that the pair were completely besotted with each another.

Although Wyatt would have liked nothing more than to think badly of the woman who had won the heart of the man he desired, he couldn't find a single negative thing to say about Claire. They'd only spoken briefly at the start of the reception, but he was a good enough judge of character to know she was perfect for Brandon.

He sighed, swirled his champagne around, and downed the drink in one go.

"Whoa there." Izzy appeared beside him, a wine glass and a plate of canapés in hand. "I think you should slow down on the alcohol."

"I haven't had that much to drink," Wyatt protested.

"That was your third champagne in the last hour," his sister said acerbically. "You know how grouchy you get when you have a hangover."

An uncommon wave of rebellion flared inside Wyatt.

"You're not my keeper, Izzy."

She narrowed her eyes at him. "Should you really be saying that to the woman who you begged to be your guest this weekend?"

Wyatt's ire faded as rapidly as it had appeared. "No. And I'm sorry." He stole a canapé from her plate and munched on it moodily.

Izzy followed his gaze to where the newlyweds and their families were laughing at something the photographer had said.

"Maybe you shouldn't have come."

"I couldn't refuse his invitation." Wyatt frowned faintly. "He's been a good friend to me ever since college. And he helped me when I set up my business."

Izzy pursed her lips. "But this is torture for you." She sighed and dropped her head on his shoulder. "I don't like to see you get hurt, Wyatt. You deserve to be happy."

Wyatt lowered his cheek against his sister's hair and wrapped an arm around her waist. "Thanks. But I kinda get the feeling love isn't gonna feature in my future anytime soon."

"You never know," Izzy muttered.

They stood in companionable silence, laughter and music from the ballroom washing over them in gentle waves. The sun was starting to set and the fairy lights strung around the gardens had started to come on, adding to the magic of the venue Brandon and his new wife had chosen for their special day.

Even though Wyatt's heart was breaking, he couldn't have wished for a better setting for Brandon's wedding. It had been a perfect weekend.

"What about you?" he said.

"What about me?" Izzy murmured.

"Is there anyone you're interested in?"

"No." A sad and oddly resigned tone underscored Izzy's voice. "I'm not really over my first love either."

Wyatt stiffened and stared at her. "What?"

Izzy rose on her tiptoes and pressed a kiss to his cheek before dragging him toward the ballroom behind them, her expression telling him she was far from ready to talk about her confession.

"Come on, let's show these folks how the Batistas dance."

Wyatt groaned as he allowed himself to be escorted inside. "Badly. We dance badly, Izzy."

Izzy laughed, the crystal clear sound drawing the gazes of several men.

Wyatt swallowed a wry smile at their expressions.

I don't think she realizes the effect she's having on these guys.

Even though she was his little sister, Wyatt was objective enough to know that Izzy was a stunning woman, both inside and out.

I wonder who she's in love with.

They danced, ate, and danced some more before Wyatt cried off and headed for the hotel bar. He was still on edge about attending Brandon's wedding and wanted something stronger than champagne to soothe his nerves tonight.

He was on his second whiskey when a man took the barstool next to him.

Wyatt glanced at the attractive blue-eyed blond. From his tuxedo, he was also a guest at the wedding. The guy ordered a whiskey on the rocks.

"Are you friend or family?" he said in a relaxed voice while he waited for his drink.

Wyatt looked at him, surprised.

The man was studying him with a faint smile.

Wyatt's belly tightened when he registered the interest in his eyes.

"I'm a friend of the groom," he said lightly. "And you?"

The man's smile widened. "I'm a second cousin of the bride." He offered Wyatt his hand. "I'm Fraser."

Wyatt hesitated before shaking his hand. "Wyatt."

They chatted lightly over their drinks. To Wyatt's surprise, it wasn't until Izzy tapped on his shoulder that he realized how late it had gotten.

"I'm pooped." She dangled her shoes from her

fingers and burped gently behind one hand. "And possibly a bit drunk. I'm going to bed."

"Sure." Wyatt straightened on his stool. "You need a hand to get to your room?"

"I'll manage." Izzy flashed a shrewd look at Fraser. "Besides, you look busy."

"Don't mind me," Fraser murmured diplomatically.

Izzy chewed her lower lip before tugging Wyatt's arm and rising on her tiptoes.

"You got condoms, right?" she whispered loudly in his ear.

Fraser made a strangled sound and turned away slightly, shoulders shaking with laughter.

Wyatt flushed. "I can't believe you just said that."

Izzy furrowed her brow. "Safe sex is important, Wyatt."

Wyatt rubbed a hand down his face. "Yes, I have condoms," he groaned. "Now, go to bed before you embarrass me further."

"Well, at least one of us is gonna get some tonight," Izzy declared brazenly before turning and heading off toward the lobby.

To Wyatt's surprise, she managed to do this in a straight line.

"It's getting late." Fraser laid a hand on Wyatt's knee. "Want to take this upstairs?" He raised an eyebrow. "No strings attached?"

A bout of nervousness danced through Wyatt as he stared at the man opposite him. Though he'd had one-night stands before, it wasn't something he'd made a habit of doing on a regular basis. He hesitated before dipping his chin.

"Let's go to my room."

To Wyatt's surprise, sex with Fraser was hot and carnal. The man was an experienced bottom and knew how to pleasure his partner in bed. As they touched and kissed and fucked and blew each other to mind-blowing orgasms, Wyatt knew this was exactly what he'd needed tonight. The physical act of lovemaking without the emotional angst that came with it. Sexual gratification without ties. The pure and simple motion of melding his body with another man's so as to fill the empty void inside him.

It was dawn by the time Wyatt collapsed on the bed, his cock pleasantly spent and Fraser's harsh pants ringing in his ears where he lay beside him, his face and chest still flushed from his latest orgasm.

As Wyatt fell into the first deep sleep he'd had in ages, he knew that he would get over his broken heart one day. And he was determined never fall in love again.

CHAPTER THREE

One Year Ago.

"Thank you for coming." Wyatt did his best to hide his tiredness behind a business smile. "I'll be in touch soon."

The woman on the other side of the desk nodded amiably and rose to her feet. "Sure thing."

The door of the office closed behind her. Wyatt sighed and glanced at the calendar on his computer.

Three more candidates, then I'm done for the day. He rubbed the back of his neck and grimaced at his stiff muscles. *Christ, who knew it would be this difficult to interview for this position.*

It was at the urging of Izzy and his closest friends that Wyatt had finally decided to hire a senior designer to come on board as his partner in *Wolf Design*. Not that he had actually advertised the position as such. He wasn't going into business with a perfect stranger without testing their skills and compatibility first.

Nearly eight years had passed since he had set up

Wolf Design. Though his parents had thought him crazy for starting his own company straight out of college, Wyatt had known there was a giant hole in the web and graphic design market in Twilight Falls and the surrounding areas of the San Bernardino Mountains. With L.A. the next closest place where potential clients could find a decent designer, it was a gap he'd been keen to fill.

His company rapidly grew from one to three, then six employees. The reputation of *Wolf Design* was such that he was now attracting a steady flow of business from L.A., his competitive pricing and flexible delivery a lure that was too hard to resist. Which is why he now found himself booked out solid for the next six months and having to work every single weekend of the previous four.

He'd considered promoting one of his current designers to the position of senior partner but had wavered when it had come to making a decision. What *Wolf Design* needed was new blood and a fresh direction.

Still, he wasn't sure if any of the people he'd interviewed so far fit that bill.

A name on the list caught Wyatt's eye. He frowned.

Of all the candidates he'd lined up today, Nathan Hardy was the one who had captured his interest the most. Not just because he'd been personally recommended by Brandon, but because of his resume.

Hardy had been a senior designer with one of the best companies on the upper west coast. He'd even won several awards for his work.

Brandon had been evasive about the reason why Hardy had suddenly left his firm a year ago. From the references Wyatt had seen, Hardy's former employers had nothing but great things to say about the man, which made Wyatt even more curious.

His cell phone buzzed. He stared at the number.

It wasn't one he recognized.

"This is Wyatt Batista."

The clamor of a busy highway traveled over the line.

"You're never gonna believe this, but my car broke down," a man said in a voice that sounded both amused and exasperated.

Lines wrinkled Wyatt's brow. "I think you have the wrong number."

There was a pause, followed by a low chuckle.

"I'm sorry, I should have introduced myself. I'm Nathan Hardy, your five o'clock appointment for the day."

Wyatt blinked. "Oh. Are you alright?"

"Yeah. I'm just waiting for roadside assistance. I wanted to let you know I'm running late."

Hardy's voice was oddly mesmerizing. Wyatt found some of his tension melting away as he listened to the man's lilting tone.

"Hello?"

Wyatt straightened. He hadn't given Hardy a reply.

"That's okay. Take your time. I'm staying late at the office tonight anyway."

"Thanks. I'll let you know when I'm on my way again."

"Sure. Stay safe."

There was a pause, followed by Hardy's slightly surprised, "Will do."

Wyatt was still staring at his cell when the next candidate knocked on the door.

"Come in."

❧

NATHAN PARKED HIS RENTAL CAR AND HEAVED A SIGH OF relief. He draped his arms over the steering wheel, propped his forehead on the soft leather, and closed his eyes.

Even though he'd started driving again soon after he'd been cleared to do so by his doctor, he still got jumpy whenever he got behind the wheel. Breaking down on the side of the highway today hadn't helped his nerves, which was why he'd been so rattled when he'd called Batista.

Let's hope the guy doesn't think I'm a complete ass after that introduction.

Nathan raised his head. He studied the pretty lights lining the sidewalk and the small park across the road before focusing his attention on the Victorian building up ahead.

Wolf Design was located on the top floor of an old, converted bank, a short walk from Twilights Falls' main street. The venue also housed several other thriving enterprises over its three floors, a sign of how much money and effort the local council had invested to make the historic town attractive to new businesses.

This was Nathan's second visit to the place. He was still as impressed as he'd been when he'd come to case the joint a few weeks back. Unlike some other tourist towns up and down the coast, Twilight Falls hadn't fallen prey to the over expansion that would have destroyed the very reason why it appealed to so many people in the first place.

It was a friend of an old college buddy of his who'd sent him the advert posted by *Wolf Design*. Having heard Nathan was possibly interested in joining a company again after freelancing for a year in and around L.A., the guy had been keen to recruit him for his company in San Francisco.

"So, I really can't convince you, huh?" Brandon Taylor had said when he'd called Nathan.

"I'm afraid not." Nathan had smiled faintly at the man's disappointed voice. "I'm not interested in signing up somewhere big." He'd looked out of the terrace doors of his rented apartment to the distant ocean. "I like it down here. The pace of life suits me."

"Have you heard of Twilight Falls?" Brandon had said after a pause.

"I have. It's a town this side of the San Bernardino Mountains, isn't it?"

"I know someone there who's looking to hire a designer. His name is Wyatt Batista. He's a good friend of mine from college. He runs a small company that is fast becoming a major player in Southern California."

Nathan had frowned faintly. "That name rings a bell."

Brandon had chuckled. "It should. He was a runner-up for several of the awards you went on to win when you just started out. And *Twilight Falls* sounds like it would be right up your alley."

Nathan had looked up *Wolf Design* after Brandon emailed him the ad for the job. He hadn't been able to find much about Batista. The guy evidently didn't like the limelight, despite how well his firm was doing.

Nathan was not someone who was easily impressed. As the top designer of his firm back in Seattle, he'd worked hard to deliver innovative projects for his clients on time, on budget, and with a level of quality that, more often than not, surpassed that of his competitors.

Wolf Design's portfolio and web presence had surprised him in spades.

It was clear why Batista was a rising star in their field. It had also become evident to Nathan why the man was looking for a senior designer.

He took a deep breath, stepped out of the car, and headed over to the building's front doors. By the time he pressed the buzzer next to the slick metal plate advertising the firm's name, Nathan felt like his calm and confident self once more.

Let's see if I'm right about my instincts.

A man's voice came through the speaker. "Hello?"

"Hey. It's Nathan."

"Come on in. The elevator's on the right."

WYATT POURED HIMSELF A FRESH CUP OF COFFEE AND glanced at his watch. He still had a couple of hours' work to do before he could call it a night. He frowned faintly.

Though he could have rescheduled the interview with Nathan Hardy, he wanted to get it out of the way today. Besides, his interest was piqued after hearing Hardy's voice. He'd found himself wondering what kind of guy was behind that captivating accent for most of the afternoon.

A door squeaked open in the main office area. Surprise danced through Wyatt.

He'd been expecting the ding of the elevator.

He popped his head out of the kitchen.

A man stood in front of the exit to the staircase. He gazed at the small reception and seating area before studying the spacious glass cubicles making up the open-plan work space of *Wolf Design* with a critical stare.

"You took the stairs?"

The stranger turned at his voice.

Wyatt blinked.

Nathan Hardy had the most piercing blue eyes he had ever seen.

Wyatt's gaze dropped.

"Oh." Nathan looked down at his outfit. "Sorry, I got engine oil on my pants. This was the only thing I had in my trunk."

Wyatt arched an eyebrow. "I've never interviewed a guy in shorts and a tie before."

A playful smile stretched Nathan's mouth. "So,

you're still gonna interview me despite how ridiculous I look right now?"

Wyatt's lips twitched. He had the feeling there was little that could faze this guy.

"Does your dress sense have any influence on your skills as a designer?"

Nathan looked at him blankly. He burst out laughing in the next instant.

"No," he said once he'd stopped chuckling. "Absolutely not."

"Good. Then, yes, I'm still gonna interview you. And you can lose the tie." Wyatt indicated his cup. "Want a coffee before we start? I just made a fresh pot."

Nathan grinned. "Sure."

CHAPTER FOUR

Nathan grabbed his wallet and keys and headed out of his house. A dark blue SUV pulled up in front just as he locked up.

"Sorry I'm running late!" Wyatt called out through the driver's window. "Izzy had an emergency."

Nathan smiled and headed down the path that bisected the pristine lawn and white picket fence surrounding his property.

"What was it this time?" he said as he climbed into the passenger seat.

"You don't wanna know." Wyatt peeled away from the curb and headed in the direction of town. "Incidentally, you've been invited to a barbecue at Alex and Finn's this weekend."

Alex Hancock was one of Wyatt's childhood friends. The lawyer had moved from San Diego to Twilight Falls in the last year to marry Finn West, an internationally renowned artist who had made the town his base. Although their relationship had started out as one of convenience, it soon blossomed into true love and the couple had recently renewed their vows in front of their friends and family.

"Those two still as loved up as ever?"

"Yeah." Wyatt rolled his eyes. "Carter and Elijah will be there too, so I'm afraid we'll have to contend with four lovesick fools." He paused. "We won't have as many PDAs with Maisie around, so that's something to be thankful for at least."

Another of Wyatt's circle of close friends, Carter Wilson was a world-famous Hollywood star born and raised in Twilight Falls. He'd chosen to make the town his home again this year, after he became the guardian to Maisie, his newly orphaned niece. It was there that he'd stumbled across Elijah Davis, a Michelin-star pastry chef who ran one of most famous bakeries this side of the San Bernardino Mountains and the man he had fallen in love with and was engaged to be married to.

Nathan knew Wyatt was truly pleased for his friends' newfound happiness despite his acerbic remarks. He grinned.

"You say that, but I bet the rest of you guys love it. Izzy sure does."

"Izzy is an irrepressible matchmaker. If Carter and Elijah aren't careful, she'll have Maisie married off before they can blink." A smug look lit up Wyatt's face. "And don't forget, they're *your* friends too now, warts and all."

"Ha ha." Nathan's gaze landed on the intricate silver

ring on Wyatt's right hand. A beautiful wolf head adorned the piece. "Is that new?"

"Yeah. Izzy had Finn design it as an early birthday present. She got it made by a jeweler he knows."

"It suits you."

"Thanks." Wyatt glanced at him. "You're settling into your new place okay?"

"Yeah." Nathan made a face. "Your realtor friend was a godsend. That house would have been snapped up in a day if it'd actually gone on the market."

"It took you long enough," Wyatt grumbled. "You made partner ten months ago. I don't know why you didn't buy a property right away."

"There was no rush." A serene feeling washed over Nathan as he looked out at the picturesque town. Though he'd only been there a year, it felt more like home than L.A., or even Seattle. "Besides, it was worth the wait."

Wyatt sighed. "I don't get how you're so laid back."

Nathan raised an eyebrow. "One of us needs to be. Our employees won't stick around if both of us are grouchy bears."

Wyatt narrowed his eyes. "Did you just call me a bear?"

"Yeah."

"I'll make you pay for that at our next poker game."

Nathan chuckled. "Bring it, Batista."

NATHAN'S LOW LAUGH DANCED DOWN WYATT'S SPINE. He clenched his hands on the steering wheel and kept a neutral expression.

He didn't know when it'd happened. When he'd started to fall in lust and in love with the man who sat next to him, oblivious to the feelings storming through him. Considering his fervent promise at Brandon's wedding that he would never lose his heart to another man, the irony of Wyatt's present situation was not lost on him.

Nathan was straight, just like Brandon.

Although Nathan wasn't in a relationship with anyone, Wyatt knew he'd dated several women since he'd moved to Twilight Falls. Most had been one-night affairs and Izzy still delighted in teasing Nathan about his apparently legendary sexual prowess and his new status as the town's most eligible bachelor.

Why the hell do I keep falling for straight guys who will never return my feelings?

It was a question Wyatt had tortured himself with a hundred times over since the day he walked into the office he shared with Nathan, took one look at the man sitting at the desk opposite his, and experienced the kind of bone-deep longing he'd only felt once before in his life.

There was no denying that Nathan was attractive. At just over six foot one, he was a couple inches shorter than Wyatt and nearly as brawny. He'd grown his hair a bit since he'd come to Twilight Falls and the dark curls now rode low on his neck line and ruffled the collar of his T-shirt. Add to this his charismatic personality and disarming smile, and Wyatt could see why the women of Twilight Falls were falling over themselves to grace his bed. Even if just for a night.

Of all of Nathan's appealing attributes, it was his eyes that still fascinated Wyatt to this day. They changed color with his every mood, going from a light sky blue when he was happy or laughing, to a midnight blue when he was irritated or focused.

Wyatt had often wondered what they looked like when he was making love. And he'd lost count of the number of times he'd imagined those piercing eyes glazed with desire and pleasure and looking up at him with passionate urgency while Wyatt thrust inside his body.

Wyatt's cock twitched as that torrid image flashed before his eyes. He gritted his teeth and thought of puppies and kittens.

There was no way he would ever let Nathan find out about his feelings. To do so would jeopardize a friendship and a business partnership he had come to value above all else.

So he would bury them, like he had done with his feelings for Brandon, and hope that one day he would get over the pain of this unrequited love too.

CHAPTER FIVE

"Uncle Nathan, can I have some ketchup?"

Nathan smiled at the little blonde girl who'd appeared at his side.

"Sure, sweetie."

He topped off Maisie's hot dog with red sauce and watched her run up to where Tristan Hart and Drake Jackson sat talking with Finn on the sundeck. She climbed back on Tristan's lap and let him prop a napkin at the top of her dress.

"Isn't it Hunter's turn to look after the grill?"

Nathan paused in the act of flipping burgers and looked over his shoulder. Wyatt was headed toward him, two beers in hand and a faint frown on his face.

"He decided to take a dip." Nathan indicated the gully beneath the terrace, where Alex and Hunter swam in the creek. "I can't say I blame him." He wiped beads of sweat off his forehead with a handkerchief and took the beer Wyatt handed him. "I might go in later myself."

The strangest expression flashed in Wyatt's eyes.

Nathan paused, his drink halfway to his mouth. He was about to quiz Wyatt when Izzy strolled out of the house. She placed a salad bowl on the table and came over with a tray of corn on the cob.

"Where's Carter and Elijah?"

"I thought they were with you," Wyatt said.

Izzy grimaced as she placed the corn on the grill. "They most definitely were not. Which means they're probably getting hot and dirty somewhere."

"Maisie is right there," Wyatt admonished in a low voice.

"I doubt she heard me. Besides, that girl has you guys wrapped around her little finger."

Nathan grinned. Maisie was happily eating her hot dog while the powerfully-built, tattooed Tristan read her a princess story book. It should have made for an incongruous image, yet it was the sweetest thing Nathan had ever seen.

"Is that why Carter had a slightly crazed look when they came over?" he drawled. "'Cause he missed Elijah?"

"Yup." Izzy took a burger from the grill and slipped it inside a bun. "He was away in New York shooting a movie for two weeks and only got back this morning." She sighed. "I pity Elijah. That guy's not gonna be able to walk tomorrow."

"Sweet Jesus," Wyatt hissed. "Can we not talk about Elijah and Carter's sex life?"

"Who's talking about whose sex life?" Hunter

dropped his towel around his shoulders and took the cooking tongs from Nathan. "Thanks, I've got this."

Izzy cocked a thumb at the house. "Carter's in there, likely ravishing his soon-to-be husband as we speak."

"Oh." Hunter grimaced. "Those two need to learn that there's a time and place for that kinda thing. Plus, it's rude to show off when most of their friends aren't getting any."

"Speak for yourself," Izzy scoffed. "And is that envy I hear in your voice?"

"Damn right it is," Hunter retorted. "At this rate, I may have to invest in a sex toy."

"That bad, huh?" Nathan said, straight-faced.

"You have no idea." Hunter gave a him a jaundiced look. "Especially you, Mr. I-have-nailed-half-the-ladies-in-town."

"That's a bit of an exaggeration," Nathan protested lightly. "I've been on five dates since I moved here."

"From the rumors, those were memorable nights indeed for the ladies in question," Hunter said sarcastically. "*Best orgasms they ever had*, apparently."

"What's an orgasm, Uncle Hunter?" someone chirped behind them.

Nathan swallowed a chortle.

Horror filled Hunter's eyes as he twisted around and looked into Maisie's innocent face. Tristan scowled where he stood holding the little girl's hand.

"You guys are despicable," the mechanic growled.

Izzy grinned. Wyatt sighed.

Carter came out on the deck, a satisfied expression on his face and a flushed Elijah by his side. Nathan patted Hunter's shoulder as the pair headed toward where the rest of them stood by the grill.

"Good luck explaining this to Maisie's dads."

"Yeah," Izzy said.

"See ya," Wyatt murmured.

"Hey!" Hunter protested as they walked off.

The rest of the afternoon passed in a pleasant whirl of laughter and conversation. It was late by the time Wyatt finally drove Nathan home.

"You guys wanna come in for a coffee?" Nathan said as Wyatt pulled up outside the quaint, white clapboard house.

"I'm good, thanks," Izzy said. "Besides, coffee's only gonna keep me up."

"Alright." Nathan stepped out of the SUV and closed the door. "Goodnight, you two."

Izzy smiled. "Night, Nathan."

"I'll see you in the morning," Nathan told Wyatt before heading up the path.

❧

WYATT WATCHED NATHAN DISAPPEAR INSIDE THE HOUSE before turning the SUV around and heading home.

He'd offered to help Nathan paint the upstairs bedrooms of his new home that Sunday. Now that he'd seen the object of his fantasies half-naked and dripping wet from a late afternoon swim in the creek, Wyatt wasn't sure that was such a great idea.

Izzy was quiet on the way back. It wasn't until they got inside their house that she finally spoke.

"Is something wrong?"

Wyatt stiffened slightly, one foot on the bottom step of the stairs.

"No. Why do you ask?" he said in a light tone.

Izzy frowned. "You look kinda distracted these days. Like you have something on your mind."

Wyatt cursed his sister's perceptiveness. She'd always been good at reading him.

"It's nothing important. Just some work stuff."

Izzy looked unconvinced. "Okay." She pursed her lips. "I'm here if you want to talk."

"I know." He headed up to his room, grateful for the brief reprieve. Knowing Izzy, she was not going to let this go.

With their parents having retired two states east, the house they'd grown up in was officially theirs. Wyatt had suggested he move out on several occasions, but Izzy would have none of it. She'd protested that the place was more than big enough for the two of them and had split the upstairs in two wings so they'd have their privacy.

To Wyatt's surprise, the arrangement had worked out better than either of them could have wished for. They'd always gotten along since they were kids and Izzy was very much an integral part of his circle of friends, having insinuated her way into their group when they got together in middle school with her now notorious determination. Not only were they each other's closest confidants, Izzy had even been the catalyst behind Alex and Finn's relationship.

But however much he loved his sister, Wyatt wasn't

ready to discuss what had been preoccupying him these past few months. A wry smile twisted his lips as he closed his bedroom door. He was aware one of Izzy's life goals was to see all of the Terrible Seven, the group of misfit kids he'd grown up with and who'd regularly terrorized their school and the town of Twilight Falls with their crazy antics, hooked up or hitched.

She can definitely count me as a failure.

He showered, brushed his teeth, and climbed into bed.

A gentle breeze made the curtains at his windows flutter as he lay with his arm behind his head. Moonlight reflected off the floor length mirror on the wall opposite the bed, casting bright shards across the ceiling.

An ache built inside him as he recalled how Nathan had looked that afternoon. Seeing the man he loved cavorting in the water, his swim shorts clinging to his powerful legs and the crystal droplets adorning his dark hair and eyelashes shining brightly under the summer sun, had been sweet torment. Nathan's skin had taken on a bronzed glow since he'd moved to Twilight Falls and the scars on his thigh and under his rib cage had looked pale against his toned, tanned flesh.

Though some men would have felt awkward about exposing their wounds, Nathan wasn't one of them. He'd been open with Wyatt and the others about the accident that had almost claimed his life two years back and that had seen him leave Seattle.

Although his tone had been light when he'd first

told Wyatt the reason for his scars, Wyatt had sensed a depth of emotions behind Nathan's words. He'd known without Nathan explicitly stating so that the incident had been a turning point in the other man's life and was likely the reason why he was so laid back. Wyatt had also realized Nathan was still nervous about driving, which is why he'd volunteered to pick him up most days on his way to work.

The ache inside Wyatt's heart slowly turned to desire. All he'd wanted to do when he'd seen Nathan all flushed and drenched that afternoon was to lick him all over until he was dry, then make specific parts of him wet and hungry for his touch. Wyatt's erection tented his pajama bottoms at the sultry images dancing across his vision. He slipped a hand inside his boxer shorts and started rubbing himself toward a much-needed release.

As he exploded on his own palm moments later, his teeth sinking into his lip to muffle his grunts of pleasure, Wyatt told himself he was a bastard who did not deserve Nathan's friendship.

CHAPTER SIX

Nathan opened his front door on Sunday morning and found Wyatt standing on his porch in shorts and a faded T-shirt.

"Hey. Thanks for coming."

Wyatt eyed Nathan's paint-streaked clothes. "You started already?"

"Yeah. I couldn't sleep because of the heat."

Wyatt moved past Nathan, his hair still damp from his shower. The smell of his shampoo teased Nathan's nose as he shut the door after him.

Oh. He changed brand.

He paused and blinked at that thought.

Wait. Since when did I care what shampoo Wyatt used?

Nathan shook his head to clear his befuddled mind and headed to the kitchen. He grabbed two bottles of ice-cold water from the refrigerator and handed one to Wyatt.

"Thanks." Wyatt unscrewed the cap and took a long, lazy swig.

Nathan stared, oddly fascinated by the way Wyatt's powerful throat muscles worked as he swallowed.

Wyatt let out a satisfied sound and wiped his lips. "By the way, Izzy said she would have come to help if she wasn't seeing Elaine today."

"That's nice of her." Nathan dragged his gaze from Wyatt's mouth and led the way to the stairs. "Are they visiting the care home?"

"Yeah. The place is having an open day. Izzy and Elaine are helping out."

Elaine was the mother of Miles Martinez, one of Wyatt's childhood friends and a member of the Terrible Seven, the group of misfits she had taken under her wings when they were but children. Miles had been in a coma ever since a tragic accident that had taken place shortly after the boys had turned eighteen and spent the past decade in a care home on the banks of Twilight Falls River, alive but unconscious. Having survived the traumatic event that nearly ended his own life two years ago, Nathan empathized deeply with Elaine.

Wyatt stopped just inside the spare bedroom.

"Maybe we should have asked the other guys to give us a hand." He studied the bare walls with a critical eye. "We'd get this done in half the time."

"Nah, I couldn't impose on them. They've got stuff to do."

Wyatt picked up a spare roller and stabbed it accusingly at Nathan.

"You realize you just indirectly insulted me, right?"

Nathan grinned, relieved they'd fallen into their

usual banter and still a bit unsure what it was exactly he'd felt just before. "You're the one who keeps saying you haven't got a life." He connected his smartphone to a wireless speaker and selected a playlist.

Wyatt groaned when country music filled the air.

"I forgot you were into this stuff."

"If you're not careful, it'll be classical music next," Nathan warned.

"What's wrong with some good old-fashioned rock 'n' roll?"

"There's nothing wrong with it." Nathan dipped his roller in the paint tray. "How about this? You pick the next playlist." He raised a haughty eyebrow. "I promise I won't bitch about it, unlike someone I know."

"Ha ha," Wyatt grumbled.

They worked in comfortable silence, Nathan occasionally humming and whistling to the songs booming from the speaker while Wyatt released the odd, long-suffering sigh. They finished painting the spare rooms by lunchtime, had sandwiches and beers in the back yard, and headed into the master bedroom in the afternoon.

"It'll be easier if we move that," Wyatt suggested after they'd done half the room. He indicated the large four-poster dominating the feature wall.

With most of Nathan's furniture still on order, it was the biggest item in the room.

"Alright." Sweat beaded the back of Nathan's neck and his forehead. "Christ, we should have done this room first," he groaned. "I forgot this side of the house got the sun in the afternoon."

Wyatt stripped out of his T-shirt. "Come on, let's do this, hot shot." The muscles in his arms and chest rippled as he dropped the material on the floor.

Nathan paused, his hands on the bottom of his own T-shirt. "Did you get bigger?" he blurted.

Wyatt blinked.

Nathan tried hard not to flush.

Why the hell did I just say that?!

A lazy smile stretched Wyatt's lips. He glanced down.

"Thanks, but I think *that* part of me stopped growing post puberty."

Nathan swallowed his embarrassment and rolled his eyes hard. "There are days when I wonder why I'm friends with you." He shrugged his top over his head and tried not feel self-conscious under Wyatt's gaze. "And I meant you look beefed up."

"I've been working out more lately," Wyatt admitted as he moved to the top of the bed.

"Oh." Nathan took hold of the bottom of the four-poster frame. "Something on your mind?"

A strange look danced across Wyatt's face. "You could say that. You ready?"

"Yeah." Nathan waited for Wyatt's signal and started to lift. Pain shot down his left thigh. He winced and sucked in air. "Wait. Let's stop for a second."

Wyatt's eyes darkened with concern as he lowered the frame. "Is it a cramp?"

Nathan nodded. He leaned against the bed and massaged his taut muscles. Though the scars from his operations had faded to thin white lines, he still suffered from the odd, crippling spasm.

"Wanna take a break?" Wyatt said.

"Nah. I'll be fine." Nathan waited until he felt the tightness loosen before straightening. "See? It's—" Something tugged on his shorts. He looked down.

The material over his hip had snagged on the intricate woodwork of the foot panel.

"Damn." Nathan twisted and tried to free himself. All he managed to do was ensnare himself farther and cause his shorts to ride down slightly on his hips.

"Wait." Wyatt came around the bed. "Let me do it." He moved behind Nathan and started working the material free. "Bear with me."

Nathan stilled when he registered Wyatt's towering presence at his back.

Has he always been this tall?

Wyatt's hot breath ruffled Nathan's hair and his nape. His fingers were equally scorching where they touched Nathan, his large hands surprisingly graceful as he untangled him.

Wyatt's thighs bumped into the back of Nathan's legs.

Goosebumps exploded across Nathan's skin at the contact. He blinked, stunned by his body's reaction to Wyatt's closeness. A muffled chuckle reached his ears a moment later, distracting him.

Nathan looked over his shoulder, not quite sure why his heart was suddenly beating just that much faster.

Shit. Bad move.

He was practically nose to nose with Wyatt.

"What was that chuckle for?" Nathan mumbled.

Wyatt grinned, his gaze focused on where he was freeing Nathan's shorts. "I was just imagining you doing this on your own. I bet you would have had to strip buck naked to get yourself out of this mess." He looked up.

Green eyes collided with blue ones. Nathan stared, mesmerized, at the specks of gold in Wyatt's irises. He'd never noticed them before.

Wyatt froze. Nathan's breath hitched in his throat.

They were close enough to kiss.

As that insane thought blasted through Nathan's mind, he saw Wyatt's gaze dart to his lips. It lasted a split second. But it was enough for Nathan to glimpse something on the other man's face. Something he'd never seen before. Something that should have scared the living daylights out of him but, for some shocking reason, didn't.

Desire.

"All done."

Nathan blinked. Wyatt's fingers grazed his hip lightly as he stepped back.

"How about we call it a day?" Wyatt rubbed the back of his neck, his eyes not quite meeting Nathan's. "You're right. It's hotter than hell up here. The paint will crack if we carry on."

Nathan swallowed a sudden bout of disappointment. "Okay."

He didn't know why he felt let down by Wyatt's shuttered expression.

Wyatt grabbed his T-shirt and headed downstairs. Nathan followed slowly in his wake.

"Thanks for lunch," Wyatt said lightly when they reached the porch. "I'll pick you up tomorrow."

"I can drive," Nathan protested.

"Your place is on my way to the office. It makes sense to carpool." Wyatt headed down the garden path and cast a detached smile at Nathan as he got inside his SUV. "Get some rest."

Nathan was still standing on his porch when Wyatt's car disappeared from view.

What was that?

Nathan walked back into the house, his mood reflective. He did some stretches, showered, and made a chicken salad for dinner. By the time he hit the sack, he still hadn't fully processed why he'd been so acutely aware of Wyatt all day or what had transpired between them that afternoon.

He knew Wyatt was gay. His business partner had been matter-of-fact about his sexual orientation and that of his friends before he'd introduced Nathan to the rest of the Terrible Seven.

Am I his type?

Nathan had never heard of Wyatt dating since he'd joined *Wolf Design*. Even when he'd taken Nathan to *The Watering Hole*, Twilights Falls' one and only gay bar, Wyatt had not flirted with any of the men who'd shown an interest in him. And there had been plenty of those.

Nathan wasn't blind to the fact that Wyatt was strikingly handsome. Though not good-looking in the classical sense, there was a brooding quality to his looks that made people look twice. And he had a body most gym buffs would die for.

Nathan frowned at the ceiling of his bedroom.

I don't know what his type is. Would he tell me if I asked him?

Warmth flooded his face in the next instant. He couldn't believe he was entertaining the idea of asking his gay business partner and friend what kind of man he was attracted to.

I must be losing my mind. What happened today was probably just my imagination. He's never expressed any interest in me that way.

Nathan ignored the feeling nagging at his subconscious, closed his eyes, and waited for sleep to claim him. Truth be told, he hadn't minded Wyatt looking at him that way. In fact, he'd been flattered. And, possibly, just possibly, a little bit curious.

CHAPTER SEVEN

He's going to be the death of me.

Wyatt's knuckles whitened on his graphic pen.

"How about brushing out those edges?" Nathan's chest pressed against Wyatt's shoulder where he leaned over his desk and pointed at the computer screen. "I think the contrast will be more interesting."

Wyatt did his best to ignore Nathan's body heat and altered the design.

"Like this?"

Nathan chewed his lip. "Hmm. Let me try something."

Wyatt's pulse leapt when Nathan clasped the back of his hand and took control of the pen. Nathan's aftershave swirled around him, an intoxicating scent that had filled his dreams more times than he could count. He hoped Nathan hadn't noticed his rising heartbeat.

This wasn't the first time his business partner had

gotten this close to him this week and it was driving Wyatt crazy.

Is he doing it deliberately? I mean, he knows I'm gay.

Nathan's fingers warmed Wyatt's skin where he worked the graphic pen. Wyatt clenched his teeth and did his best to think of innocuous things rather than the fact that the man he desired was close enough for him to touch and kiss.

Thank God I haven't got a hard-on. He swallowed a groan. *I don't think I could look him in the eye if he saw I was aroused.*

Nathan straightened a moment later, a satisfied smile on his face.

"There. I think that's better."

Wyatt had to concede that Nathan had improved on his design.

He'd been right on the money when he'd appointed Nathan as a senior designer a year ago and asked him to partner with him a few months later. Nathan's energy and flair had reinvigorated *Wolf Design* and stopped them from heading down a path that would eventually have rendered their brand stale, something Wyatt had begun to fear. Working with Nathan was both fun and challenging, even if they did not always agree on things.

He startled when Nathan laid a hand on his shoulder.

"Bet you're glad you have me, huh?" Nathan drawled.

Wyatt twisted in his chair and arched an eyebrow.

"Did you just compliment yourself?"

Nathan grinned. "I did. I think I'm pretty awesome, actually."

"You are." Wyatt's mouth stretched into a teasing smile. "Still, I think your ego needs taking down a notch or two. Maybe we should change our next game night to strip poker. I think having you buck naked might be an appropriately humbling experience."

❧

NATHAN'S HEARTBEAT STUTTERED AT WYATT'S WORDS. Having engaged in his own personal game of poke-the-bear the whole week, it was both thrilling and daunting to witness the reactions of the man he'd deliberately been goading.

He hadn't failed to notice how Wyatt's breathing and pulse had picked up when he'd touched him. Not had he missed the other little ticks that confirmed his suspicion that Wyatt was interested in him romantically.

"*Sooo*, what you're saying is you wanna see me naked, huh?"

Wyatt propped an elbow on his desk and looked Nathan up and down. He rubbed his chin thoughtfully. "Maybe."

It took all of Nathan's effort not to gulp. The look in Wyatt's eyes was definitely predatory right now.

"But don't get your hopes up," Wyatt added. "We tried it once when we were drunk and it didn't end well."

Nathan blinked. "You guys played strip poker before?"

Wyatt grimaced. "Like I said, it didn't end well. Izzy walked in on us."

Nathan snorted. "Don't tell me. She took pictures."

Wyatt stared. "Oh. You knew?"

Nathan's eyes rounded. "No. It was a wild guess!"

Wyatt scratched the back of his neck. "Well, she did. And she's still holding them over our heads."

"Wow. Izzy is one scary chick."

"Don't say that to her face. You'll live to regret it."

The tension between them melted away as they smiled at each other.

"Wanna get lunch?" Nathan said.

"Sure. Why don't we go to Elijah's place? He was going to try a new savory pastry this week."

They checked in on the rest of their staff before heading out of *Wolf Design*.

"Want me to help you paint the rest of your place?" Wyatt said as they strolled into town. "We should be finished early today."

Nathan hesitated. "That would be great, thanks."

He knew he was tempting fate by having Wyatt over again so soon after last weekend's incident, but he was now more intrigued than ever by Wyatt's interest in him.

They slowed when they turned a corner and came in sight of Elijah's bakery. There was a queue outside *La Petite Bouche Gourmande*.

"You'd think that guy was a rock star instead of a pastry chef," Wyatt muttered.

"He's not just anyone, though." Nathan grinned. "Didn't some world-famous Michelin star chef come chasing after him when he first opened up his bakery?"

"Yeah. Carter was pissed about that."

Sam Harris, the bakery's manager, spotted them through the window when they joined the line. She came to the entrance and poked her head out of the door.

"What are you guys doing?"

"We're waiting our turn," Wyatt said in a slightly defensively tone.

Sam sighed. "You know Elijah gets upset when you pull that polite shit. Get in here." She flashed a dazzling smile at the other customers. "I'm sorry ladies and gents, but these guys are VIPs."

The women murmured among themselves, their expressions appreciative as they eyed Wyatt and Nathan.

"Wow," Nathan said when the line parted. "I feel like we're on a red carpet."

"Shut up and walk faster," Wyatt grumbled.

Sam guided them to a table and took their orders.

"Elijah busy in the back?" Wyatt said when she came over with their drinks.

Sam pulled a face. "That's one way to put it. He's practically having to sit to work." Her lips grew pinched. "Carter is a beast. I fear for Elijah's virtue."

"I'm pretty sure Elijah lost that a while ago," Wyatt said drily.

Nathan chuckled. Sam's gaze shifted to him.

"Speaking of which, I haven't heard any juicy stories about you for a while."

"I don't know what you mean," Nathan said innocently.

Sam rolled her eyes. "Oh, please. I've heard tales of your expertise in the bedroom. So, you going through a dry spell? The ladies are starting to talk."

Nathan stirred his lemonade with a straw. "Let's just say I'm…considering my options."

Surprise flashed in Wyatt's eyes.

Sam grimaced. "Options, huh? I would love to pretend I'm not jealous about the fact that you have *options*, but that would be a barefaced lie." Someone called her name. "I'd better go. Your food will be ready soon."

"You're thinking of dating someone?" Wyatt said after Sam had left their table.

Nathan faltered. He'd only been half lying when he'd told Sam he was considering his options.

I can hardly tell him he's the only option I'm thinking of these days.

The fact that he was even considering what it would be like to go out with Wyatt would have shocked everyone who knew Nathan from his former life in Seattle. He'd been a ladies' man since he could walk and talk and had gone out with more than his fair share of women after he started dating in high school. He'd only had a handful of long-term relationships in the past, but none after he'd broken up with Melissa. Since he wasn't ready to commit to anyone, one-night stands had become pretty much par for the course after he moved to L.A. and Twilight Falls.

It was the promises Nathan had made to himself after he left Seattle that had been at the forefront of his mind since he'd become aware of Wyatt's interest in him.

He'd vowed that he would live his life to the fullest and do things he'd never dared do in the past. That he would embrace new experiences and fresh ways of thinking. That he would not be boxed into a particular lifestyle or ethos.

Going out with a man was not something he'd ever contemplated before.

And sleeping with one would normally have been so far outside his comfort zone he didn't think the old him could ever have imagined it even in his wildest dreams.

But this was Wyatt. A man he strongly admired. Someone he liked not just as a business partner, but as a companion. Someone who was dear to him.

Friends falling for each other was as old as time. It was what had happened with him and Melissa after all, although their parents had actively encouraged that relationship.

Having spent the last week egging Wyatt on, Nathan knew he now had a decision to make. Wyatt was most definitely interested in him. It was also clear he did not intend to act on his feelings. Which left Nathan with two options.

He could either elect to respect Wyatt's unspoken wish or he could choose to challenge it.

As he gazed at the man across the table from him, Nathan realized he had already made his choice. Even though the prospect scared the hell out of him and he was about to tread previously uncharted territories, he could not walk away from Wyatt. He pursed his lips.

Now, how does a guy go about asking another guy out on a date?

CHAPTER EIGHT

Wyatt finished making a bowl of salad and had just placed a couple of marinated steaks in a skillet when the doorbell rang. He strolled out of the kitchen and headed down the hall to the front door.

Nathan was standing on the porch, a couple of six-packs in hand and a lazy smile on his face.

"You're early." Wyatt narrowed his eyes. "Also, you thanking me for helping paint your house should involve you cooking for me, not the other way around."

Nathan came in and handed him the drinks, his expression unabashed.

"I thought we could get a beer in before we ate. And we both know you're the better cook." He sniffed the air appreciatively. "Is that steak I smell?"

"Yeah." Wyatt led the way to the kitchen. He took a couple of beers from one of the six-packs, put the rest in the refrigerator, and finished seasoning the steaks.

"Where's Izzy?" Nathan said curiously as he set the table.

"She had a business meeting in San Francisco. She's spending the night with some friends she knows up there."

"Oh. I would have brought less booze if I'd known she wasn't going to be here."

Wyatt seared the meat and placed them in the oven before popping the cap on his bottle. "You might as well stay over if we're intending to drink all of it."

Nathan took a swig of his own drink and raised an eyebrow.

"Why, are you planning on getting me drunk, Mr. Batista?" he said in a teasing voice.

Wyatt stared. He could have sworn Nathan had just tried to flirt with him.

I must be tired. There's no way he'd do that.

"We both know you have a scarily high alcohol tolerance," Wyatt said drily. "You even drank Drake under the table that one time."

Nathan grinned. "That I did."

They sat down to eat and chatted about work and their plans for the weekend. By the time they finished washing up and headed into the TV room, they were on their third beer.

"Boy, I'm pooped." Nathan dropped down heavily on the couch. "That was really nice."

"It was only steak and salad. Not exactly gourmet food." Wyatt sat beside him and reached for the remote control.

"You overestimate my cooking skills."

"Right. I forgot I was talking to the man who once

burned a boiled egg." He selected a movie channel. "What do you want to watch?"

"You pick. I'll probably nod off halfway anyway." Nathan winced and rubbed his left thigh. "Mind if I sit on the floor? I need to stretch my legs."

"Take the couch." Wyatt moved down onto the floor.

"You sure?"

"Positive."

They'd finished their drinks and were a third of the way into the movie when Wyatt realized he'd made the wrong choice. What had started out as an action flick had turned into an endless sex fest. It didn't help that the alcohol was making him lightheaded or that the male actor looked a bit like Nathan.

Wyatt put his empty bottle on the coffee table, hyperconscious of the man behind him. Nathan's right leg brushed against Wyatt's back where he'd stretched out on the couch.

Wyatt did his best not to stare at the body of the movie star on the screen. He pretty much knew what Nathan looked like under his clothes, bar what was inside his boxers. The guy on the screen had nothing on him.

"I wonder if they get aroused when they act out those scenes," Nathan mused.

Wyatt blinked.

"It must happen, right?" Nathan added. "I mean, they're naked and touching and kissing."

Wyatt suppressed a groan.

Any more talk like this and I'm pretty certain I'll be the one getting aroused.

"So, what do you think?" Nathan asked insistently.

"I—don't know."

"Hmm." Nathan paused. "But we *do* know someone who does though."

Wyatt cast a warning look at Nathan over his shoulder, all thoughts of how provocative the other man was being flying out of head.

"We're not asking Carter if he gets hard when he's filming his sex scenes," he said stiffly.

Nathan grinned. "You're such a party pooper."

Wyatt's gaze flitted to Nathan's mouth.

Shit.

He swallowed. "Want another beer?"

"I'll get it." Nathan made to sit up.

"No." Wyatt climbed to his feet. "You stay put."

Besides, this will give me a chance to cool my head.

Nathan relaxed back down on the couch.

"You're spoiling me. If this continues, I'm going to expect you to carry me upstairs, princess style."

Wyatt stared. There was no mistaking the light in Nathan's eyes.

He's definitely flirting with me.

Wyatt clamped down on the sudden awareness crawling across his skin.

"If I'm going to carry you, it'll be over my shoulder."

Nathan's pupils flared at that.

Something sparked between them.

Heat pooled in the pit of Wyatt's stomach. He

turned and headed out of the room, hands shaking and heart thumping against his ribs.

What was that?!

The flash of sexual attraction he'd just felt from Nathan had his mind reeling. Wyatt clenched his jaw and grabbed a couple of beers from the refrigerator. He hesitated before swapping one of them for a bottle of water.

I better stop drinking. I have no idea what he's up to, but I need my wits about me.

By the time Wyatt regained his composure and returned to the TV room, Nathan was fast asleep. Something that felt a lot like disappointment shot through Wyatt. He put the drinks on the coffee table.

"Nathan?"

Nathan did not stir.

Wyatt rubbed the back of his neck ruefully as he studied the man on the couch.

Looks like I was worrying for nothing. It must have been the alcohol after all.

He switched the TV off and went in search of a blanket. He didn't want to wake Nathan up and the couch was more than comfortable enough for him to sleep on.

Wyatt left a light on in the corner of the room and locked up. He was about to head upstairs when he decided to check on Nathan one last time.

A familiar ache tugged at his heart when he stopped next to the couch and looked down at the sleeping man. Wyatt lowered himself on his haunches, his hungry gaze roaming Nathan's relaxed face in the faint, golden light.

Nathan shifted under the blanket. A lock of hair fell over his eye.

Wyatt reached out and moved the stray strands. He froze when he realized what he'd just done.

Nathan's breathing remained slow and steady.

Wyatt hesitated before grazing Nathan's cheek gently with his knuckles, powerless to resist touching the man he desired. His fingers bumped against the corner of Nathan's mouth. He swallowed.

Get up. Walk out of this room right now, before you do something you'll really regret.

Wyatt ignored the voice screaming inside his head and leaned down. He brushed his lips softly across Nathan's.

Desire slammed into him, hot and demanding.

He fisted his hands where he rested them on the edge of the couch.

Stop. Enough.

Nathan's eyes fluttered open.

"Wyatt?" he mumbled sleepily.

Wyatt's stomach dropped.

Oh God.

Nathan closed his eyes and went back to sleep.

Wyatt waited breathlessly, his heart racing with trepidation. When it was clear Nathan was not going to wake up, he rose and walked out of the room, his legs trembling and remorse twisting his belly.

CHAPTER NINE

"Seriously, what's gotten into you?" Izzy stared. "You've been like a bear with a sore paw all weekend."

Wyatt bit back a sharp retort. Izzy was right.

"I'm sorry." He finished buttering his toast and munched moodily on his breakfast.

Izzy glanced at the clock on the kitchen wall.

"Aren't you going to be late picking up Nathan?"

"I told him I couldn't give him a lift today," Wyatt murmured, not quite meeting her eyes.

Izzy frowned. "That's new. You guys are usually glued at the hip."

"Yeah, well, we aren't."

Izzy dumped some jam on her warm croissant and studied Wyatt thoughtfully over the pastry. "Does this have to do with whatever's been bugging you lately?"

Wyatt swallowed a curse. He took his plate and coffee cup, rose, and headed over to the sink. "I really don't have time for this."

"Did something happen between you and Nathan?"

Izzy's question made Wyatt freeze in his tracks.

Damn it.

He kept his back to his sister and washed up briskly, his silence filling the room.

"I'm right, aren't I?" she said doggedly.

"I'm leaving." Wyatt dried his hands and made for the exit.

"Don't think this conversation is over, young man," Izzy said sternly as he walked out of the kitchen.

"I'm older than you," Wyatt snapped over his shoulder.

He took his wallet and keys from the table in the hall and stormed out of the house. Guilt stormed through him as he started his car.

I really am behaving like an asshole. To Izzy. His hands tightened on the steering wheel. *And to Nathan.*

A sudden summer shower was pelting the town when he parked down the road from *Wolf Design*. By the time Wyatt entered the foyer of the building, he was drenched to the skin. He gazed anxiously at the heavy drops hitting the blacktop outside and found himself regretting his decision not to pick Nathan up.

Will he be okay driving in this?

Wyatt took the stairs to the third floor two steps at a time and hurried into the reception.

"Hey, Adam. Is Nathan here yet?"

Relief flooded him when *Wolf Design*'s receptionist and secretary nodded.

"He got here five minutes ago." A puzzled look dawned on the young man's face. "Don't you two normally come together?"

"There was a change of plans," Wyatt muttered.

He ran a hand through his damp hair and crossed the open plan floor to his and Nathan's shared office, his T-shirt and jeans clinging uncomfortably to his skin. He kept a spare gym bag and clothes at work, so at least he didn't have to go home to change and face Izzy's wrath.

Wyatt vaguely noted that the privacy glass had been activated as he opened the door. He took a step inside and rocked to a standstill, the air leaving his lungs just as effectively as if he'd been sucker punched.

Nathan stood in his boxer shorts and little else by his desk. His hands stilled on the towel he was using to dry his hair.

Their eyes locked across the room.

Nathan broke the silence first.

"I see you got caught in the rain too, huh?"

He finished rubbing his hair and reached for the neatly folded T-shirt and jeans on the table.

A bittersweet emotion clogged Wyatt's throat when he registered Nathan's light tone.

"Yeah." He tore his gaze from Nathan's muscular arms and six-pack and went over to his desk.

This was the first time they'd spoken since the weekend.

To Wyatt's surprise, Nathan appeared to have no recollection of their kiss when he'd woken up on Saturday morning. He'd greeted Wyatt normally and even helped make breakfast before he left. Though they'd had plans to watch a baseball game on Sunday afternoon, Wyatt had canceled at the last minute, the guilt he'd felt at having stolen a secret kiss from Nathan still too raw in his mind.

Wyatt took his spare gym bag from under his desk and rooted inside.

"Damn," he muttered a moment later.

"What is it?" Nathan said.

"I thought I had a towel in here."

"Here. Use mine." Nathan lobed his towel across the room.

Wyatt caught it and hesitated.

Nathan sighed. "It doesn't have cooties, Wyatt."

"Sorry." Wyatt kicked his shoes off, stripped out of his wet shirt, and was unbuckling his jeans when he felt Nathan's gaze on him. His hands froze on his belt.

Nathan was studying him with the strangest expression.

"Nathan?"

"Oh." Nathan startled. He turned and put his wet clothes away, his movements jerky. "Sorry, I didn't mean to stare. Do you want a drink?"

"Sure." Wyatt waited until Nathan had left the room before stripping and drying off, the scent of Nathan's body wash enveloping him. By the time Nathan returned with two cups of steaming coffee, he was dressed and had concluded that he'd imagined Nathan's flustered tone a moment ago.

❧

NATHAN WALKED OVER TO HIS DESK AND SAT DOWN. HE turned his computer on, opened his calendar, and scrolled through his to-do list, careful not to look at the man across the room from him.

He'd seen Wyatt half-naked plenty of times before, including when they'd swam in the creek behind Finn and Alex's house.

Yet, his heart had never pounded as hard as it was doing right now.

He'd never looked at another man's body in a sexual way before. Nothing could have stopped him from staring at the hard lines and angles of Wyatt's torso and arms when the latter had stripped out of his shirt just now, or wondering how that rock-hard body would feel against his own.

He felt heat flood his cheeks at that last thought.

Wyatt in wet clothes should be illegal.

Wyatt's hair was still damp where he sat behind his desk.

Nathan glanced at him surreptitiously over his monitor and fought the urge to go over and run his hands through the thick, dark curls to see if they were as soft as they looked.

Now that he'd resolved to seduce Wyatt, Nathan couldn't help zeroing in on his captivating little habits. Like how Wyatt arched his left eyebrow when he was being sarcastic or how his cheeks dimpled sexily when he smiled. Or the way he bobbed his right knee slightly when he was concentrating and how his eyes darkened to a forest green when he became passionate about something.

Truth be told, Nathan found himself utterly mesmerized by Wyatt.

So, he's gonna pretend that kiss never happened, huh?

When he'd woken up on Wyatt's couch on Saturday morning, Nathan had realized his attempt to flirt with the man had failed miserably. There had been a moment when he'd felt a definite sizzle of chemistry between them, but he'd fallen asleep before he could explore it further.

Nathan thought he'd dreamt the kiss Wyatt had given him at first. The way Wyatt had acted since that night had raised his suspicions that it hadn't in fact been a dream. And after witnessing Wyatt's reaction just now, Nathan was convinced it had really happened.

He fought the urge to touch his mouth. He couldn't believe he'd missed fully experiencing the first kiss Wyatt had given him. From what he recalled, Wyatt's lips had been featherlight, as if he'd been scared to press them to Nathan's.

Well, I was asleep.

The sense of disappointment Nathan experienced after he realized Wyatt was never going to admit to the act worsened as the morning wore on. By the time evening came and he and Wyatt parted ways, Nathan knew the other man remained determined to bury his feelings for him.

Irritation blossomed inside Nathan as he drove home. He scowled through the windshield.

We'll just have to see about that, Batista.

CHAPTER TEN

"Straight Flush." Tristan smiled triumphantly and placed his cards on the table. "Read it and weep, suckers."

Groans erupted around the kitchen.

"Every single time," Alex grumbled.

"Amen," Drake concurred.

"Hey, he won fair and square," Hunter protested.

"You wouldn't be saying that if we were playing for real money," Carter said. "That guy would have stripped us of our homes and the clothes on our backs by now."

Tristan looked unabashed.

"I'm surprised you made it tonight," Nathan told Carter. "Weren't you shooting a movie in New York?"

"I've got the next ten days off." Carter sighed. "Thank God, otherwise I would have dragged Elijah and Maisie there with me."

"Have you thought about what you'll do when you guys get married?" Wyatt said. "Elijah can't leave his bakery business for days on end and Maisie is going to preschool."

Carter made a face and ran a hand through his hair. "I have. I won't be able to quit my acting career for a while yet, but I'm talking to some friends who want to open a studio about coming on board as a producer in the future."

This earned Carter a battery of stares.

"You're thinking of quitting acting?" Hunter said, shocked.

Drake frowned. "It's what you've always wanted to do."

A rueful smile stretched Carter's lips. "I never imagined I would want to stop this soon either, but my priorities have changed. I love acting, but I cherish my life with Elijah and Maisie more."

"I don't get that," Drake muttered in the silence.

Alex narrowed his eyes. "That's because you've never experienced true love."

"Yeah, well, if true love makes you do crazy things, then I don't want to," Drake said darkly.

Wyatt bit back a sigh. All of them knew Drake and Alex had had a fling in the past. Though things had been tense between the two men when Alex first returned to Twilight Falls, they'd since patched things up. Alex now seemed determined to find Drake his happy-ever-after, just as he'd found his with Finn.

Between Izzy and him, I don't know who's the most trouble.

Izzy came home from a night out with her girlfriends just as they finished their final game.

Although she'd quizzed him all week, Wyatt had remained tight-lipped about what had happened between him and Nathan. He intended to put the kiss he'd stolen from his friend and business partner firmly in the past. Talking about it would only twist a knife in the wound in his heart.

Nathan hung back and helped him tidy up after the other guys had left and Izzy had gone upstairs to her room. To Wyatt's relief, the awkward tension he'd sensed between them all week hadn't manifested itself tonight.

Nathan seemed back to his normal self.

"Want a coffee before you head home?" Wyatt said after they'd finished clearing the kitchen.

"Sure."

Wyatt put the coffee pot on and got a couple of mugs out of a cabinet. He was conscious of Nathan's pensive gaze on him where the latter leaned against the counter, his arms folded across his chest.

"So, you're really not going to talk about it, huh?" Nathan murmured.

Wyatt glanced at him, puzzled. "Talk about what?"

"The kiss."

Wyatt froze. His heart started a heavy drumming inside his chest. He turned his head mechanically and met Nathan's eyes.

"I know you kissed me last Friday, Wyatt," Nathan said quietly.

THOUGH HE WAS DOING HIS BEST TO SOUND CALM, Nathan's pulse raced wildly as he looked at the man standing a short distance from him.

After spending the last few days thinking about the situation between him and Wyatt, Nathan had come to the conclusion that the only way for them to move forward was to get Wyatt to admit that he liked him.

If this meant using guerrilla tactics, then so be it.

The haunted look filling Wyatt's eyes made Nathan want to walk over and wrap his arms around him. He dug his nails into his palms and resisted the urge to comfort the man who'd been running from him all week. Wyatt might as well have been standing on the moon so large was the rift Nathan suddenly felt between them.

Nathan's stomach twisted in knots as he studied Wyatt. He hadn't grasped how painful it would be to see Wyatt deny his feelings for him.

"You knew?" Wyatt said hoarsely, his eyes dark with guilt and regret.

"To be honest, I thought I'd imagined it at first," Nathan admitted. "But the way you've been acting since that night confirmed it wasn't just a dream."

Wyatt swore and raked a hand through his hair.

"I'm sorry," he blurted, his voice full of anguish. He gazed beseechingly at Nathan. "Can you please forget about it? It was a mistake. I was drunk and—"

"No, I won't," Nathan interrupted. "I don't want to forget, Wyatt. About the kiss or your feelings for me."

Wyatt stared at Nathan as if he'd sprouted a second head.

"What?"

"I know you like me," Nathan said. "Romantically."

Wyatt paled.

Nathan finally closed the distance between them. He took the coffee pot, poured their drinks, and handed a mug to Wyatt.

"What I'm saying is we need to talk about this." He went over to the table. "Because, I gotta tell you, I'm pretty pissed about the fact that you've been hiding how you feel for God knows how long."

Wyatt hesitated before joining him. He took the chair opposite Nathan, as if he wanted to put some physical distance between them.

"Are you gonna quit *Wolf Design*?" he said roughly.

"No." Nathan gripped his mug hard, fear suddenly coiling through him. "Do you want me to?"

"No!" Wyatt denied vehemently.

A fraught silence filled the kitchen.

"What did you mean when you said you were angry about me—" Wyatt faltered, "hiding my feelings for you?"

"I meant just that. I'm upset that you've kept this to yourself for—" Nathan waved a hand vaguely. "How long has it been anyway?"

"Three months, two weeks, and five days," Wyatt replied promptly.

Nathan blinked. "That's kinda precise."

"Sorry," Wyatt murmured.

Nathan frowned. "Stop apologizing."

Wyatt's fingers whitened on his mug. "I don't get you. You're straight. Surely, having a gay guy lust after you isn't something you want? Aren't you… disgusted?!"

Nathan took a sip of his coffee and told himself to keep his cool. Imagining Wyatt getting hot and bothered over him was doing all kinds of surprisingly wanton things to his heartbeat and his libido.

"So, you've been lusting after me?"

Some color returned to Wyatt's face. "Really? That's what you're choosing to focus on right now?!"

Nathan shrugged. "I'm curious."

Wyatt's lips grew pinched. He raised his drink.

"In your fantasies, do you top me or do I top you?" Nathan said, keeping his tone light.

Wyatt froze, his mug halfway to his mouth. "You're kidding me right now?"

Nathan smiled. "Nope. I've never been more serious."

Something seemed to snap behind Wyatt's guarded facade.

"You really want to hear about the fantasies I have about you?" he grated out.

A shiver danced down Nathan's spine at the untamed light that flashed in Wyatt's eyes.

This is the side of him he's been hiding from me. The side of him that wants me.

"Yeah, I do."

"Alright. But don't say I didn't warn you." Wyatt downed his coffee in one go and placed his mug on the table with a thump. "The answer to your question is that I top you. In all my fantasies, I'm the one who fucks you, not the other way around. In reality, I could probably try bottoming for you, but I'm very much a pitcher. And I want inside you so bad I've lost count of the number of times I've masturbated while thinking about making love to you in the past few months."

Nathan's heart thumped violently as Wyatt's words brought a flood of torrid images to his mind.

"Tell me more," he breathed.

Wyatt's pupils flared at his husky command. A sudden stillness came over him, as if he were handling a dangerous animal.

"In one of my fantasies, I blindfold you with a red silk scarf and take you on all fours from behind. In another one, I sit you right here on this table and suck you until you're bone dry and shuddering with pleasure."

Nathan's belly clenched.

"I've taken you in every position a man can take another man," Wyatt said harshly. "I've kissed you, rimmed you, blown you until you practically fainted, fucked your mouth with my cock, and made love to you from dusk to dawn."

"Oh God," Nathan mumbled.

Wyatt's expression grew shuttered. "Heard enough?"

"I'm kinda turned on right now."

Wyatt blinked. "What?"

Nathan groaned. "I'm sorry to have to tell you this, but I don't find anything you've just said disgusting. It's hot as hell and it's making me hard."

CHAPTER ELEVEN

Wyatt gaped at the man opposite him.

Is he for real?!

Nathan's face was flushed and his eyes slightly glazed as he looked at Wyatt.

"None of this grosses you out?" Wyatt stated in disbelief.

"Trust me, my dick is definitely not grossed out right now."

Wyatt shifted in his seat, his own groin growing uncomfortably tight.

"So, what you're saying you wanna go out with me?" he said warily, still not sure what to make of this conversation.

Never in a million years could he have imagined that he and Nathan would be sitting down one day and talking so calmly about the fact that Wyatt liked him.

Nathan narrowed his eyes at his incredulous tone.

"You sound like I'm proposing we commit a criminal act."

"You're straight," Wyatt blurted out.

"That has nothing to do with it."

Wyatt frowned. "That has everything to do with it. You're not into guys!"

"Well, I'm apparently into you," Nathan retorted.

Wyatt's heart stuttered. He couldn't stop the sudden blind hope rising inside him. He squashed the foolish feeling firmly.

He was wishing for something that would never happen.

"We're business partners, Nathan," Wyatt said stiffly. "I don't want to jeopardize our working relationship. Or our friendship, for that matter."

"I've thought about that and I have a solution," Nathan said doggedly. "Carter and Elijah are getting married in five weeks. I propose we consider the time between now and their wedding as a trial period. If it doesn't work out, we turn back the clock and pretend none of this ever happened."

Wyatt clenched his jaw. Though he was widely tempted to accept Nathan's insane proposition, he knew it would only lead to heartache.

"I don't think that's a good idea."

Nathan's brow furrowed. "Why not?"

"Because—" Wyatt stopped and swallowed. "Because I'll only end up falling for you more and I'll be miserable as hell when it's over."

Nathan's pupils flared at his husky admission. He took a moment to digest Wyatt's words.

"So, what you're saying is you're a coward."

Wyatt's eyes widened. "What?"

"You're a coward, Wyatt." Nathan's tone had turned razor sharp. "You're so scared of losing that you're giving up before you even try."

The storm of feelings sweeping through Wyatt morphed into anger.

"I'm being the voice of reason, Nathan," he snapped. "While you're being a rosy-eyed fool!"

"What's wrong with being an optimist?" Nathan countered.

"There's a difference between blind optimism and being a realist!" Wyatt growled.

"That's where you're wrong." Nathan's eyes were a dark, midnight blue as he glared at Wyatt. "I told myself after I woke up from my accident that I would embrace life. That I would do things I've never done before. I've lived by that motto for the last two years. And I'm telling you I want to give this a try."

A buzzing sound filled Wyatt's ears. He gazed blindly at Nathan, bitterness suddenly choking his throat. "Is this what this is, Nathan? A bucket list? You want to say you fucked a man before you die?!"

Nathan fisted his hands on the table. "I'm trying really hard not to come over there and punch you right now."

Heated silence filled the room as they glowered at one another.

"I don't want to live my life with regrets, Wyatt," Nathan said in a determined voice. "I have too many of those already. And I'm telling you right now that both of us will regret not taking this chance."

Wyatt rubbed his hands down his face and blew out a sigh, the fight suddenly draining out of him.

"Do you even realize what having sex with a man entails?"

Nathan's expression grew cautious. "I've been reading up on it."

Wyatt swallowed a groan.

He's killing me right now.

Nathan pursed his lips. "Let me make something clear. I have a high pain threshold, but that doesn't mean I like pain. So, I hope you'll—you know," he paused and scratched the back of his head awkwardly, "prep me well. I mean, I don't want to have my virgin butthole ripped open by your magnum."

Wyatt gaped. A burst of shocked laughter escaped him.

"I can't believe you just said that," he managed between chuckles.

Nathan smiled. "It's true. First sign of pain and I'm outta there."

The heaviness that had been weighing on Wyatt's heart and mind since the day he realized he was in love with Nathan finally started to lift.

"So, how do we propose we go about this?"

Nathan blinked, as if the question had taken him by surprise.

"Well, I guess we should go on a date."

Wyatt smiled faintly. He had a feeling dating Nathan would be a helluva lot of fun.

"But I want to try something first," Nathan added.

Wyatt looked at him, puzzled. The words Nathan

said next took the wind out of his sails and sent blood surging to his groin.

"I want to kiss you."

Wyatt's pulse hammered erratically in his veins. "Like, *now*?!"

Nathan nodded. He pushed his chair back and rose to his feet.

Wyatt stood up as Nathan came around the table. He stayed still, curious as to what Nathan would do. Nathan stopped in front of him. His ears and cheeks held a hint of color that told Wyatt he wasn't as cool and collected as he was making himself out to be.

Wyatt's lips curved in a faint smile. "You look nervous."

"Am not," Nathan mumbled.

"We don't have to do this right—"

The rest of Wyatt's words died in his throat when Nathan clasped his face and kissed him.

Their teeth clashed. Wyatt choked on a snort.

Nathan pulled back and narrowed his eyes. "Did you just laugh at me?"

"I'm starting to doubt your reputation among the ladies."

"Ha ha." Nathan's fingers clenched on Wyatt's jawline. Determination filled his face. "Okay, I'm going in."

"That's a funny way to put—"

Wyatt's thoughts scattered to the winds when Nathan molded their mouths together. Nathan stared at Wyatt as he slowly explored his lips, his own soft and hot where they touched Wyatt's. Nathan's eyes darkened to indigo.

Oh God. This isn't happening. I must be dream—

Nathan slipped his tongue inside Wyatt's mouth.

Wyatt's mind went blank. Hunger exploded inside him. He gripped Nathan's wrists and returned the kiss, his tongue wrapping commandingly around the intruder exploring the inside of his mouth.

Damn. He tastes good!

Nathan made a throaty sound of appreciation. He moved closer to Wyatt.

Wyatt dropped his hands to Nathan's waist. He leaned back against the table, parted his legs, and pulled Nathan into the cradle of his thighs.

Nathan came willingly, his attention focused on where their tongues mated sensuously, his chest heaving with his quickening breaths.

He stiffened when Wyatt's erection bumped against his groin.

Wyatt froze, the desire swirling inside him dampened by Nathan's sudden stillness.

This is where he's gonna realize he can't do this after all.

Nathan drew back slightly and looked down.

"That's not a magnum." He stared at Wyatt's straining cock. "It's a bazooka."

Wyatt blinked before bursting out laughing. He pressed his forehead against Nathan's, the relief surging through him so profound his arms shook slightly as he hugged Nathan.

"I think we should call it a night," he mumbled in

Nathan's hair once he'd stopped chuckling. "Anymore more than this and I don't know what I'll do to you."

"You mean, you might lose control and have crazy monkey sex with me?"

Wyatt felt Nathan smile where he pressed his face against Wyatt's throat.

"That and more."

Nathan shivered. Wyatt swallowed.

He knew it wasn't fear that was making the man in his arms tremble. And that scared him more than anything in the world.

CHAPTER TWELVE

Nathan willed away the butterflies swarming his stomach and studied his reflection in the hallway mirror.

It was Sunday night and Wyatt was on his way to pick him up for their date. For the first time in his life, Nathan had spent nearly half an hour in front of his closet debating what to wear. He'd finally settled on cream chinos, a navy dress shirt, and tan brogues.

A knock came at his front door. Nathan picked up his wallet and keys from the table in the hall, took a deep breath, and opened it.

His pulse jumped when he saw the man standing outside.

Oh, wow. Has he always been this hot?

Wyatt's imposing figure was bathed in the glow of the porch lights. He was wearing gray jeans, a charcoal blue T-shirt, and a somewhat nervous look. His pupils flared when he saw Nathan's outfit, his apprehension replaced by admiration.

"You look nice."

The butterflies in Nathan's belly multiplied at Wyatt's husky voice.

"Thanks. So do you."

Wyatt's T-shirt hugged his broad chest and muscular arms, while his jeans highlighted his strong thighs. Nathan did his best not to stare.

Damn. I can't wait to see how his ass looks in those.

Nathan blinked at that illicit thought.

Though he'd seen Wyatt practically every day for the last year, tonight felt like the first time he was *really* looking at him. And the guy was one mighty fine feast for the eyes. He cleared his throat to hide his nerves.

"I gotta say, I'm kinda disappointed."

Wyatt's face fell. "Why?" He looked down at himself. "Is this too casual?"

"No. Your clothes are perfect. It's just, well," Nathan shrugged, "I was expecting flowers."

Wyatt blinked. "You wanted flowers?"

Nathan grinned. "I'm kidding." He sobered when he saw Wyatt's keen expression. "Like, seriously. If you turn up on my doorstep with a bouquet, I'm gonna pretend I don't know you."

Wyatt sighed at his threat.

"Has anybody ever told you you're an incorrigible tease?" he muttered while Nathan locked up.

"Plenty of people have."

Nathan glanced surreptitiously at Wyatt's back as they strolled down the path to the SUV. He grinned.

Yup, his ass looks great in those jeans.

"So, where are we going?" Nathan asked in a voice

that he hoped masked the filthy direction his thoughts had just taken.

"I booked us a table at that new place outside town."

Nathan arched an eyebrow as he climbed in the passenger seat.

"You mean the fancy restaurant that looks out over the river?"

"Yeah."

"I'm impressed. I heard they had a two-week waiting list."

Wyatt closed his door and started the car. "Izzy knows the owner." He pulled away from the curb.

"Oh." Nathan hesitated. "Does Izzy know about—?" He waved a hand vaguely between them.

"What, that we're dating? No, I haven't told her yet." Wyatt glanced at him. "Would it bother you if I did?"

Nathan heard Wyatt's hidden question behind the one he'd voiced.

"It wouldn't." He paused. "And I don't mind if you tell the other guys either."

Wyatt looked surprised at that. "You don't?"

"Nope."

"Hmm." Wyatt gazed thoughtfully through the windshield.

"What was that '*hmm*' for?"

"I might keep this from the guys for the time being."

Nathan couldn't squash the disappointment rising inside him.

Is he ashamed of me?

He did his best to keep his tone neutral. "Why?"

Wyatt shifted uncomfortably in his seat and mumbled something.

"I didn't hear that," Nathan said.

"I said I don't want to tell them 'cause I'm pretty sure a couple of them fancied you at some point."

Nathan sucked in air, his dismay fading as fast as it had appeared. "They did?!"

"Yeah," Wyatt said darkly.

Nathan bit the inside of his cheek. He could hardly tell Wyatt that he found his disgruntled tone and expression totally adorable.

"So, who had the hots for me?"

Wyatt's brow furrowed. "You're enjoying this, aren't you?"

Nathan grinned. "I can't say I'm not."

Wyatt blew out a sigh. "Drake and Tristan."

Nathan raised his eyebrows, a little taken aback. "You're kidding? Those two? *Really*?!"

"Yup."

Nathan was silent for a while. He would never have guessed Drake and Tristan had been interested in him.

"Gay guys really have the ultimate poker faces, huh? What about Hunter?"

"What about Hunter?"

"Am I not his type?" Nathan said doggedly.

Wyatt frowned. "Hunter has someone on his mind right now."

"Oh."

Wyatt gave Nathan a stern look. "You sound disappointed."

"I do?"

"Yeah," Wyatt practically growled.

Nathan arched an eyebrow. "Are you jealous?"

Wyatt's hands clenched on the steering wheel. "Yes."

Nathan's pulse fluttered at his heartfelt admission.

"Does that scare you?" Wyatt said gruffly.

"No." Nathan rubbed the back of his neck, his ears suddenly warm. "It's…kinda hot, actually."

Wyatt studied the road ahead with an intense look, braked, and pulled onto the hard shoulder.

Nathan gave him a puzzled look. "What are you—?"

Wyatt undid his seat belt, leaned across the console, and took Nathan's mouth in a heated kiss.

Nathan gasped. His heart thumped violently when Wyatt slipped his tongue inside his mouth. Nathan hesitated for the briefest moment before returning the kiss just as passionately, desire swirling through him.

He was still getting used to how different it felt to do this with a man. The hard lines of Wyatt's bristled jaw. His body heat. The commanding way he mated their tongues together.

All of it was new and shockingly exciting.

Wyatt's fingers clenched where he held Nathan's face. He wrenched their mouths apart and pressed his forehead against Nathan's, his hands trembling on Nathan's skin.

"I'm sorry," Wyatt blurted. "I just—I just had to kiss you."

He moved back, clipped his seat belt in, and headed onto the road.

Nathan gazed blindly ahead and fought the urge to touch his lips. His mouth still tingled and his body throbbed from the ardent kiss he and Wyatt had just shared. Nathan blinked, startled by a sudden realization.

He hadn't wanted Wyatt to stop.

"We're here," Wyatt said.

Nathan looked out of the window just as Wyatt turned off the road and headed down a driveway to a secluded parking lot. Visible through the woods beyond was a pretty, brightly-lit building straddling the banks of Twilight Falls River.

CHAPTER THIRTEEN

Wyatt took a sip of his water and did his best to calm his frazzled nerves. He could feel the curious stares of the other diners on them.

He'd thought the restaurant would be quiet tonight but had failed to account for its popularity. There wasn't a single empty table in the place and it was packed wall to wall with couples.

Nathan seemed oblivious to the attention they were drawing where he sat drinking a glass of wine opposite Wyatt.

"You decided on what you want?"

Wyatt startled. He looked at the menu and forced himself to focus.

"I'll have the lobster."

"Good choice. I think I'm gonna have the steak."

A waitress came over to take their order.

"And how would you like your meat, sir?" she asked Nathan politely.

"Medium rare." Nathan's gaze locked onto Wyatt's. "And…juicy."

The look in Nathan's eyes went straight to Wyatt's dick. He swallowed a groan, grateful that their table sported a floor length sheet. He didn't think the other diners would have missed his growing erection otherwise.

"Did that innuendo loosen you up a bit?" Nathan drawled once the waitress left.

"Kinda," Wyatt muttered.

"Good. 'Cause you've looked pretty tense since we walked in here." Nathan looked around the restaurant before studying Wyatt with a shrewd expression. "Are you always this self-conscious when you're out on a date?"

Wyatt's fingers tightened on his napkin.

"I don't usually go out on dates," he admitted reluctantly.

Surprise widened Nathan's eyes. "When was the last time you went on one?"

Wyatt bit back a sigh. He didn't really want to reveal to Nathan that he'd never dated anyone for a significant period of time.

"I don't remember."

Nathan stared. He looked around furtively to make sure no one was within earshot and leaned across the table.

"Does that mean you haven't had sex in a while either?" he said in a low voice.

Wyatt closed his eyes briefly, not sure whether it

was frustration or exasperation he was experiencing right now.

He's not gonna let this go, is he?

"I'm not a monk, Nathan. I know where I can find guys who just want a one-night stand."

Nathan's eyes darkened. He licked his lips, his expression strangely intense.

Wyatt's dick twitched. "What's that look for?"

"I really want to see your 'O' face right now," Nathan confessed.

Wyatt groaned out loud. The sound drew the stares of the couple at the next table.

"You're killing me," Wyatt muttered once the pair had gone back to eating their meal.

"Well, they do call an orgasm the 'little death'—"

Wyatt leaned across the table and pressed a hand to Nathan's mouth.

"I'm not gonna be able to walk out of here if you keep that up," he growled.

Nathan's pupils widened. Wyatt's heart stuttered.

It wasn't just surprise he was reading in Nathan's eyes. Nathan was thrilled to hear Wyatt was hard for him.

Wyatt swallowed a curse and snatched his hand away.

Nathan had just licked his palm.

Why, this little—

"Yup," Nathan declared with a self-satisfied smile. "Definitely gotta see that 'O' face."

Wyatt wasn't sure how he made it through dinner. He'd been right when he'd surmised that dating Nathan would be a hell of a lot of fun, with emphasis on the 'hell' part. The guy was a thorough tease and Wyatt's cock barely survived the sexual innuendos he kept slipping into their conversation.

It was ten by the time they headed out of the restaurant, Nathan looking sated and Wyatt wishing it wasn't just the food and alcohol that was making him so.

There were plenty of things he wanted to do with Nathan that would satisfy them both.

"Wanna head home?" Wyatt said as they crossed the parking lot.

Nathan arched an eyebrow. "Moving a bit fast there, aren't we, stud?"

Wyatt flushed. "I didn't mean it that way."

Nathan smiled. "I know. And no, I don't want to go home. Let's go for a drink at *The Watering Hole*."

To Wyatt's relief, the bar wasn't as busy as the restaurant and they found a table near a window. Wyatt went to fetch their drinks and was making his way back when he came across Drake.

"Hey," Drake greeted from where he sat at a high table.

"Hey yourself." Wyatt acknowledged the man next to Drake with a faint nod. The guy looked vaguely familiar.

Drake glanced at the beer and water in Wyatt's hands before looking around the bar. He spotted Nathan by the window. "Is it just the two of you?"

"Yeah," Wyatt replied evasively.

"Why don't you introduce me to your friend?" The guy next to Drake was eyeing Wyatt appreciatively.

If Drake was aware of his date's interest in Wyatt, he showed no indication of it.

"Wyatt, this is Jerry. Jerry, Wyatt."

"Nice to meet you," Wyatt murmured. He looked at Drake. "See yo—"

"Wanna join your friend and his partner?" Jerry interrupted. He looked keenly from Wyatt to Drake.

Drake shrugged. "I don't mind—"

"No," Wyatt said vehemently.

Surprised flashed on Drake and Jerry's faces.

Shit.

Wyatt's knuckles whitened on the bottles in his hands.

"Sorry. Nathan and I are having a late business meeting."

The expression in Drake's eyes told Wyatt he'd seen through his barefaced lie. "No problem. I'll catch you later."

Wyatt felt Drake's gaze on his back as he headed for his and Nathan's table.

"Was that Drake?" Nathan said curiously.

"Yeah."

"Isn't that one of the local DJs with him?"

Wyatt looked over his shoulder.

Jerry smiled and waved at them coquettishly behind Drake's back.

"Oh. That's why he looked familiar."

Nathan took a sip of his beer and glanced around the bar.

"It's funny," he said after a moment.

Wyatt studied him curiously. "What is?"

"I never thought I would come here on a date with you."

Wyatt's pulse accelerated slightly. A faint smile stretched Nathan's lips and his blue eyes fairly twinkled as he gazed at Wyatt.

He's so goddamn sexy.

Nathan's pupils dilated slightly.

"I can't help but feel that you're thinking of something really dirty right now."

Nathan's husky voice danced hotly across Wyatt's skin. Wyatt swallowed and took a deliberate gulp of his water.

Nathan arched an eyebrow. "That filthy, huh?"

His smile widened. He looked around before leaning back in his chair.

Wyatt heard a soft thud under the table. The next thing he knew, Nathan's foot was grazing his shin.

Wyatt clenched his hand around his water bottle.

"What are you doing?" he said stiffly.

"I'm just checking something."

Wyatt bit back a groan as Nathan's toes brushed up his left knee and thigh.

He's testing the limits of my sanity.

He froze when Nathan stroked his erection lightly.

"Fuck." Wyatt's knuckles whitened on his drink as his dick jerked in pleasure.

Nathan's lips parted and his breathing accelerated. "You're hard as steel."

Wyatt reached down and gripped Nathan's bare ankle.

"You're playing with fire, Nathan," he grated out.

Nathan flexed his toes. Wyatt sucked in air.

"You're right," Nathan breathed as he kneaded Wyatt's erection. "Your dick is burning up."

Wyatt heard the final thread of his patience snap.

That's it!

CHAPTER FOURTEEN

Nathan gasped when Wyatt pushed his chair back, grabbed his hand, and hauled him to his feet. He barely had time to slip his foot back in his shoe before Wyatt dragged him toward the exit.

A wild thrill shot through Nathan when Wyatt cast a scorching glance at him over his shoulder.

Uh oh. The bear is definitely awake.

The lust darkening Wyatt's eyes should have unnerved Nathan. Except it didn't. It was turning him on so bad his dick was doing press ups behind his chinos.

To Nathan's surprise, Wyatt tugged him past his car, skirted the parking lot, and took him around the side of the bar. He found a secluded corner between two outbuildings, pushed Nathan against the white clapboard wall, and crowded him in.

"You're really good at getting me riled up, you know that?" Wyatt growled inches from Nathan's mouth.

Nathan's heart thumped hard at the untamed look

in Wyatt's eyes. Wyatt's arms grazed his head where he'd braced them on either side of Nathan. It was the only part of him touching Nathan. Yet, it felt like he was caressing Nathan's body with feverish hands.

"I'm turned on too."

Wyatt's eyes flared at Nathan's softly spoken admission. He looked down and cursed when he saw Nathan's bulging erection. His lips landed on Nathan's with a hunger that took Nathan's breath away.

Wyatt yanked Nathan's wrists above his head, parted Nathan's legs with his thigh, and went to town on Nathan's mouth.

Blood buzzed and pounded in Nathan's ears as Wyatt kissed him with savage passion. He'd always been the one in control when he'd made love to women and had wondered if this would pose a problem when it came to dating Wyatt. After all, Wyatt had made it clear that he wanted to top him and intended to be the physically dominant partner in their trial relationship.

But it seemed like Nathan had been worrying for nothing.

Wyatt's scent. His taste. His heat.

All of it was sweeping Nathan up in a whirlwind of desire that had him panting and trembling. He didn't care who was making love to whom.

A strangled sound of pleasure escaped him when Wyatt massaged his cock with his thigh.

"Do you like that?" Wyatt murmured hotly against Nathan's lips.

"Do you even have to ask?!" Nathan groaned.

"Show me," Wyatt commanded. He looked down to

where he was torturing Nathan's erection with his hard flesh, the material of his jeans rubbing Nathan's cock with the sweetest friction. "Let me touch you." His eyes locked back on Nathan's. He nipped at Nathan's lower lip with his teeth. "Can I, Nathan?"

In that moment, Nathan knew Wyatt could have asked him for anything in the world and he would willingly have surrendered it. No one had ever looked at him the way Wyatt was looking at him right now.

Desire. Love. Lust. Adoration.

Wyatt's gaze burned with it all and more.

Nathan swallowed before nodding shakily.

Wyatt kissed him hard before dropping a hand between their bodies. The clunk of Wyatt unfastening his belt and the rasps of their zippers being pulled down brought heat to Nathan's face. Whatever embarrassment Nathan was experiencing vanished when Wyatt grazed his knuckles across his cock.

Nathan's hips bucked instinctively, seeking the touch of the man who was driving him out of his mind. He looked down just as Wyatt caressed his taut belly and dipped his fingers inside his boxers. Nathan couldn't have stopped the lustful sound that climbed up his throat even if he'd wanted to when Wyatt touched his bare flesh.

"Ah!"

Wyatt's harsh breaths echoed in Nathan's ears as he fondled Nathan's erection, his clever fingers caressing and squeezing Nathan's sensitive skin with an experienced touch. Nathan shuddered when Wyatt freed him from the tight confines of his underwear. He watched, mesmerized, as Wyatt moved his wicked hand up and down his rock-hard organ.

"Shit!"

Wyatt let go of Nathan's shaft and hastily freed his own dick from his jeans. Nathan's eyes glazed over.

He really is *big!*

He hissed when Wyatt closed a hand around both their cocks and started rubbing them briskly, his palm slick with their pre-cum.

Wyatt nudged Nathan's chin up with his nose and took his mouth in a frantic kiss. He pushed Nathan flush against the wall, one hand still holding Nathan's wrists prisoner while he jerked them off with the other.

"You feel so damn *good!*" Wyatt growled, breaking their kiss. He jerked his hips in a way that had Nathan biting down hard on his own lip.

Nathan leaned forward, blindly seeking Wyatt's mouth again. Wyatt obliged eagerly, his lips crashing against Nathan's and his tongue invading Nathan's mouth with an ardent mastery that had Nathan's legs trembling.

Wyatt planted his feet firmly on the ground and started rolling his hips in a sensuous dance that had their swollen cocks bumping and grinding together.

"Wyatt!" Nathan groaned.

All coherent thought fled Nathan's mind at the sinful feel of Wyatt's burning flesh rubbing intimately against his own.

He had never felt this way before.

This frenzied feeling. This desperate yearning for release.

He felt like he would self-combust if he didn't come and soon.

Nathan stared beseechingly at the man making love to him with his mouth and hand, begging for something only he could give him.

Wyatt's eyes flared. He squeezed Nathan's shaft and moved his thumb in lazy circles across the head of Nathan's cock.

Nathan's orgasm raced down his spine and tightened his belly. He rose on his tip toes as his balls contracted with exquisite tension. It took everything he had to keep his eyes open when he climaxed seconds later, his grunts of pleasure muffled by Wyatt's demanding lips, his dick spilling his seed in Wyatt's eager hand.

Wyatt's pupils dilated until they were dark circles of ecstasy. His whole body stiffened and his face flushed as his orgasm swept over him. He groaned and shuddered against Nathan when his cock exploded, his hips pumping fitfully against Nathan's. Nathan bit back a hiss when Wyatt's hot cum splashed across his stomach.

He wanted to see it.

He wanted to watch Wyatt's cock pulse and throb with pleasure.

He wanted to touch and smell Wyatt's musky essence where it coated his own dick and belly.

But he couldn't tear his gaze from Wyatt's face.

It was some time before both of them stopped

shuddering where they leaned against one another. A warm buzz of contentment filled Nathan as he closed his eyes and pressed his face against Wyatt's shoulder. He could feel Wyatt's heart thundering where their chests touched.

"I was right," Nathan mumbled.

"About what?" Wyatt panted in his hair.

"Your 'O' face. It was amazing."

Wyatt's body quaked with silent laughter.

Nathan smiled. Convincing Wyatt to take a chance on them had been the right decision after all. Not only did they have terrific sexual chemistry, they also cared deeply for one another. And he was pretty sure the fuzzy feeling in his heart wasn't just an afterglow of the pleasure he had just experienced in Wyatt's arms.

CHAPTER FIFTEEN

"WHAT'S THIS ABOUT?" IZZY SAID CURIOUSLY.

"I want you to help me choose a birthday gift for Wyatt," Nathan stated.

Izzy's eyes widened with surprise. Nathan masked a frown.

Looks like he still hasn't told her we're going out.

A week had passed since his and Wyatt's first date. Despite the torrid kisses they'd shared that night and the unforgettable hand job Wyatt had given Nathan, they'd managed to keep their interaction at work normal the following day.

They also hadn't kissed since that night. This state of affairs would have frustrated Nathan had they not been facing a deadline a client had suddenly sprung on them and which had had their entire team working late most of the last week.

It was Saturday morning and Nathan had asked Izzy out for coffee. He studied her thoughtfully as he stirred his drink.

Maybe he just didn't find time to talk to her.

Nathan still hadn't fathomed why it was important to him that Wyatt be open about the fact that they were dating. Truth be told, he'd assumed that it would have been the other way around. That he would be the one who'd want to keep their trial relationship a secret.

Nathan hadn't missed the longing looks Wyatt had given him when he'd thought he wasn't looking these past few days, nor had he been unable to stop himself from doing the same. Not being able to touch one another in the last week had only ramped up the sexual attraction burning between them.

It was clear their secret would not remain one for long.

"I would have thought you of all people would know what my brother wants for his birthday," Izzy said, her expression inquisitive. "He spends more time with you than anyone else in Twilight Falls, including me."

Nathan felt his ears grow warm at Izzy's assertion.

She's kinda right.

Nathan knew what Wyatt wanted. He just wasn't sure if he was ready to give it to him yet.

An image flashed before his eyes.

Of him, naked and with a bow tied around his dick.

Nathan bit back a wry smile.

Yeah, he would definitely love that.

"I was thinking of buying him a watch," he said lightly. "You've already given him that ring though."

"I doubt he'd mind if you get him more jewelry." Izzy grimaced. "I originally intended to get him a tuxedo for Carter and Elijah's wedding, but he saw me looking at online catalogues and banned me from getting one."

Nathan froze, his coffee halfway to his mouth.

Now he was imagining himself naked on a bed with a bow tied around his dick and Wyatt slowing stripping out of a tuxedo and climbing on top of him.

Great. I've been reduced to having day time fantasies about the guy I just started dating.

"You okay?" Izzy said. "You have the strangest look on your face right now."

Nathan did his best not to flush. "Yeah, I'm fine."

The door to the coffee shop jangled.

"Oh. There's Drake." Izzy waved the other man over.

Drake went to get a drink and joined them. "What are you guys up?"

Izzy grinned and cocked a thumb at Nathan.

"He finally succumbed to my charms and asked me out on a date."

Nathan stiffened. Drake's face grew shuttered.

"It was a joke," Izzy groaned at their expressions. "Sheesh, what is with you two?" She rose. "I'm going to the ladies. I hope both of you are acting normal by the time I get back."

Awkward silence fell between Nathan and Drake after Izzy left.

Nathan ran a hand through his hair. He had a strong suspicion Drake knew he and Wyatt had been on a date the night he'd seen them at *The Watering Hole*.

"Is there really nothing going on between you and Izzy?" Drake said.

"No, there isn't. I asked her out so she'd help me choose a gift for Wyatt's birthday."

"Shit." Drake stared. "That's in two weeks, right?"

Nathan raised an eyebrow. "You mean, you forgot?"

"Yeah." Drake scratched a stubbled cheek. "I'm awful at birthdays. Hunter normally reminds me." Faint lines furrowed his brow. "It seems he's got other things on his mind these days." He studied Nathan thoughtfully. "What are you getting Wyatt?"

"I was thinking of buying a watch from this new designer in L.A. Izzy already had a ring designed for him by Finn. She said Wyatt probably wouldn't mind having the watch too."

"He won't," Drake said. "He likes his jewelry, even though he doesn't wear a lot of it." A shrewd light lit his eyes as he sipped his coffee. "Hmm. A watch would make a great gift."

"Hands off the watch idea," Nathan warned.

Drake smiled faintly.

The tension between them slowly melted.

"I'm sorry," Drake said gruffly. "I'm the last person who should be judging others, but I don't want to see Wyatt get hurt."

Nathan gazed at him steadily. He'd only recently heard from Wyatt about the complicated relationship between Drake and Alex, and how it had almost ended Alex's marriage with Finn.

It seemed Drake still hadn't forgiven himself about that.

"Thanks. I appreciate your honesty."

Drake raised an eyebrow. "So, you two are really going out?"

Nathan smiled faintly. "Is that so hard to believe?"

"Kinda," Drake replied bluntly. "You're straight."

"Well, I gotta admit, the idea of having my virgin butthole ravaged by a huge dick still unnerves me, but I'm willing to give it a shot," Nathan drawled.

Drake choked on his coffee. A shadow loomed over their table.

"Who's getting his what ravaged by what?!" Izzy hissed where she stood behind them.

Heads turned at the nearby tables.

"Great." Nathan gave Izzy a stern look and pointed at her chair. "Sit down."

"Man, that cat practically dove out of the bag," Drake mumbled, wiping his mouth.

"You're not helping," Nathan snapped.

Izzy took her seat and studied them with a shrewd stare. "So, you guys are fucking?"

This one earned them wide-eyed looks from the other customers.

"No!" Nathan barked.

"Jesus, Izzy," Drake muttered.

"Then what?" Izzy said, undaunted. "And I thought you were straight." This she directed at Nathan.

"He is," Drake said. "He and Wyatt are dating."

Nathan inhaled sharply. Izzy sucked in air.

Drake shrugged at Nathan's disapproving scowl.

"What? It's not as if it was gonna remain a secret for

long. This is a small town and you guys are not exactly being discreet."

Nathan swallowed a retort.

He's right.

Understanding dawned on Izzy's face. "Is that why Wyatt's been acting so strange lately?"

Nathan's ears perked up. "Strange how?"

"Like something's been weighing on his mind. And he's been grouchy as hell."

"Sexual frustration does that to a man," Drake drawled.

"Ah." Izzy's expression cleared. She arched an eyebrow at Nathan. "You guys haven't done the dance of the two-headed beast yet?"

"We just went on our first date," Nathan declared haughtily.

Izzy and Drake stared.

"You're saying you don't like to put out until the third date?" Izzy said carefully.

"I didn't take you for a prude, considering your reputation with the ladies," Drake murmured.

"I'm not a prude," Nathan protested. "It's just—" He rubbed the back of his neck, embarrassed. "I don't want to mess this up. And I definitely don't want to hurt Wyatt."

Izzy grew quiet. "You really are serious about my brother?"

"Yes."

"Good. 'Cause I'll be the first to punch your lights out if you break his heart."

Nathan registered Izzy's steely tone. "I have no intention of doing that."

"Still, it's pretty dicey, considering you two are business partners," Drake said.

"We decided to give it five weeks," Nathan explained. "We'll decide on Carter and Elijah's wedding whether to continue this relationship or—"

"Or end it?" Izzy said stiffly in the silence that followed.

Nathan dipped his chin.

"That's the stupidest idea I've ever heard," Drake said flatly.

"Look, it was the only way I could convince him to give this a try!" Nathan snapped.

Surprise dawned on Izzy and Drake's faces.

"Wait. *You asked Wyatt out?!*" Izzy squealed.

"I take back the bit about you being a prude." Drake's eyes glinted with admiration as he studied Nathan.

"Wyatt is stubborn. He was never going to tell me that he liked me." Nathan frowned. "He even kissed me when I was sleeping and begged me to forget it ever happened."

Izzy gasped. "*He didn't?!*"

Drake frowned. "It didn't freak you out? Being kissed by another man?"

"No." Nathan hesitated. "I don't know how I would have felt if it had been anyone else but Wyatt though."

"You love him," Izzy whispered.

Nathan blinked. Heat flooded his face. His heart contracted with a mixture of fear and hope.

"I—I don't know," he stammered.

Izzy raised a hand. "It's okay. You don't have to say anything." Her expression turned apologetic. "That was too forward, even for me."

Nathan looked blindly into his coffee.

Is this what this feeling is? He swallowed. *Am I falling in love with Wyatt?*

"Well, if I were Wyatt, I know exactly what I would want for my birthday," Drake declared confidently.

Izzy nodded.

Nathan eyed them warily. "You guys are thinking of something really dirty right now, aren't you?"

"Yup," Izzy said. "You naked, with a bow wrapped around your dick."

"Bingo," Drake murmured.

Color rushed to Nathan's face.

Izzy's eyes rounded. *"Oh my God! You were thinking the same?!"* she screeched, her hands rising to her flushed cheeks.

Nathan and Drake hushed her.

CHAPTER SIXTEEN

Wʏᴀᴛᴛ ᴘᴀʀᴋᴇᴅ ᴏᴜᴛsɪᴅᴇ Nᴀᴛʜᴀɴ's ʜᴏᴜsᴇ ᴀɴᴅ ᴛᴜʀɴᴇᴅ the SUV's engine off. A fine summer drizzle was falling across Twilight Falls and clouds obscured the evening sky. He put the hood of his jacket up and jogged up the path to the porch, a wine bottle in hand.

Nathan's faint shout reached him when he knocked on the front door.

"Come on in! It's open!"

Wyatt went inside the house and closed the door behind him.

Nathan popped his head out of the kitchen at the end of the hall, his expression strained.

"We may have an emergency."

Wyatt smiled faintly. He could smell something burning. "Is that our dinner?"

"Yeah." Nathan chewed his lip worriedly. "I have no idea where I went wrong. I swear I followed Elijah's recipe to the letter." He disappeared from view.

Wyatt bit back a chuckle and headed down the

hallway. As he'd suspected, his second date with Nathan was going to be just as entertaining as their first.

He faltered slightly when he recalled Izzy's saccharine grin as he was leaving the house. Though she hadn't said anything, he couldn't help but feel she knew what was going on between him and Nathan. Wyatt sighed.

I really should talk to her.

He stopped just inside Nathan's kitchen and examined the damage.

Cooking utensils were strewn haphazardly across the worktop. Something was smoking in the casserole dish on the range.

Wyatt took his jacket off, dropped it on the back of a chair, and rolled up the sleeves of his dress shirt.

"Is that beef bourguignon?"

"Uh huh," Nathan said in a miserable voice where he stood stirring the pot.

Wyatt eyed the apron around Nathan's waist and neck and reluctantly added the item to his never-ending list of fantasies about the man.

It's a miracle I don't have a permanent erection around him.

The memories of their first date were still fresh in Wyatt's mind and had been the subject of many a hand job since that night. He and Nathan hadn't touched or kissed each other after their torrid session outside *The Watering Hole*, the rest of their week taken up by a deadline sprung on them by one of their regular clients. They'd even had to forgo their regular poker game with the other guys on Friday and it wasn't until Sunday that they'd finally managed to meet up outside work.

Nathan had insisted on making dinner for their second date.

"Why don't I see if I can rescue this?" Wyatt took the wooden spoon from Nathan's hand. "Are we having mashed potatoes and green beans?"

Nathan nodded morosely. "We were supposed to."

Wyatt studied the mangled remains of the vegetables on the cutting board and bit the inside of his cheek.

Nathan narrowed his eyes. "You're laughing at me, aren't you?"

"I am not," Wyatt said in a strangled voice. "Do you have a bread maker and flour?"

"I do," Nathan said sullenly.

Wyatt leaned over and kissed the tip of his nose. "Why don't you get them out and open the wine?"

Nathan flushed slightly before nodding, his fingers rising to touch the spot where Wyatt had kissed him. It was clear he wasn't used to being the recipient of such intimate gestures. Wyatt fought the urge to take him in his arms right there and then, and ravish his mouth.

He hadn't been sure what to expect when he'd turned up at Nathan's place tonight. He knew Nathan wasn't ready to go all the way with him yet and he had no wish to rush that aspect of their relationship either. Wyatt wanted Nathan's first experience of penetrative sex to be as perfect and as painless as he could make it.

But there were plenty of other things they could do to make out before then.

Wyatt was still mulling this over when they sat down for dinner a while later.

"I have no idea how you did it," Nathan declared in open admiration as he stared at the meal laid out on the table before them. "And I was watching you the whole time."

Wyatt poured them a glass of red wine and raised his in a toast.

"Something tells me you weren't focusing on my cooking," he said wryly.

Nathan clinked his glass against Wyatt's and took a sip of the alcohol. "You can't exactly blame me. My boyfriend is kinda hot."

Nathan's teasing words burned Wyatt's ears and went straight to his groin.

Wyatt clamped down on his libido. "Am I your boyfriend?"

Nathan's pupils flared slightly at Wyatt's husky voice. "Uh huh."

Wyatt's dick stiffened to attention.

Shit.

He glanced at the food. "Maybe we should skip dinner and go straight to dessert."

"That would be a waste after all the effort you put in making it." Nathan arched an eyebrow. "And why do I get the feeling you're talking about a different kind of dessert to the cake I picked up from Elijah's place?"

"You can't blame a guy for trying," Wyatt said bluntly.

Nathan rolled his eyes, lifted his fork, and pointed it at Wyatt.

"Patience is a virtue, Mr. Batista. Now, let's eat."

Though his tone was admonishing, his gleaming gaze told Wyatt he was curious to see what Wyatt had in mind for them later that night.

Wyatt wasn't sure how he managed to make it through the meal. By the time they finished eating, he was wound tighter than a spring and ready to explode. He could tell from the hint of color staining Nathan's cheekbones and the pulse thrumming at the base of his throat that he wasn't immune to the sexual tension swirling between them.

Wyatt barely tasted the coffee and cake they had for dessert. When Nathan rose to clear the table, Wyatt followed him and crowded him against the sink.

He knew he was rushing things but he needed to touch Nathan. Now.

"Leave it." Wyatt closed his arms around Nathan's waist from behind and pressed a hot kiss to his nape.

Nathan shuddered and dropped his head forward, exposing his skin to Wyatt's hungry lips. "We should really—"

Wyatt whirled him around and took his mouth in a demanding kiss.

Ah. Finally. I've been waiting all week for this!

Nathan's sweetly addictive taste washed over Wyatt's tongue as he deepened the kiss. Nathan groaned and wrapped his arms around Wyatt's neck, his tongue meeting Wyatt's in a passionate clash of hot flesh. The way Nathan pressed his body against Wyatt's told him he was just as eager for this as Wyatt was.

Wyatt dropped his hands to Nathan's waist and backed him out of the kitchen and into the sitting room, his mouth plundering Nathan's in never-ending, scorching kisses.

Nathan's breath whooshed out of him when Wyatt wrenched their mouths apart and pushed him down on the leather couch. His pupils were inky pools in a sea of midnight blue as he looked up at Wyatt, his cheeks flushed and his chest heaving.

Wyatt parted Nathan's thighs with his hands and knelt in front of him.

"I want to taste you."

The way Nathan's breath hitched in his throat told Wyatt he really liked that idea. Wyatt ran his knuckles lightly down Nathan's erection, his torrid gaze locked on Nathan's own glazed one.

CHAPTER SEVENTEEN

Nathan sucked in air and bucked his hips, stunned by the electric feel of Wyatt's touch. Tonight felt different than their first date. The air between them was hot and heavy, so much so Nathan was finding it difficult to breathe.

It was as if Wyatt was finally showing him the dark depths of his desire for him.

"Can I, Nathan?" Wyatt leaned down and pressed a soft kiss to Nathan's stiff cock through his jeans. "Taste you?"

Nathan shivered, his dick pulsing in response.

Damn! He's gonna make me come without actually touching me!

Nathan hesitated before nodding shakily, unable to deny the man looking at him with such bone deep hunger. He couldn't wait to find out what Wyatt's mouth would feel like on his bare flesh.

Wyatt's eyes darkened. He stripped Nathan of his T-shirt and jeans and shrugged his own shirt off his broad shoulders, his movements swift and uncontrolled. Nathan shuddered when he registered Wyatt's enormous erection.

Wyatt leaned up, cradled Nathan's face in his hands, and took his mouth in the softest, most reverent kiss Nathan had ever received.

The contrast to the fierce desire sizzling between them was so sharp Nathan could only moan. Wyatt's gaze burned as he stared into Nathan's glassy eyes, his lips and tongue moving slowly and seductively against Nathan's.

Nathan wrenched his mouth from Wyatt's a moment later, overcome with emotion.

"Wyatt!" he gasped.

Wyatt bumped his forehead lightly against Nathan's, his expression gentle despite his scalding gaze, as if he could sense the turmoil raging inside Nathan's heart and soul.

"Tell me, Nathan," he breathed. "Tell me what you want me to do to you."

Nathan closed his eyes. He couldn't help the stab of fear that shot through him then.

He had never experienced so many powerful feelings in such a short time. The sweet joy of Wyatt's tender kisses. The frenzied craving his hungry ones ignited inside him. The bottomless passion and lust he could feel radiating off the man holding him.

Wyatt's desire was threatening to swallow him whole and Nathan wasn't sure if he could survive the storm sweeping over them both.

"Do you want me to stop?"

Wyatt's words had Nathan's eyes snapping open. "No!"

Wyatt blinked at his vehement denial. He studied Nathan for a silent moment before touching Nathan's cheek gently with his knuckles.

"Are you scared?" he said quietly.

Nathan gulped before dipping his chin.

A painful expression danced across Wyatt's face. He started to pull away. "I'm sorry. I'll—"

Nathan's stomach twisted. "Don't!" He clutched at Wyatt's shoulders. "Just—just give me a minute."

Wyatt watched him cautiously, as if he were a wild animal about to bolt.

"I—I feel like I'm about to lose myself in you," Nathan mumbled.

Wyatt's eyes widened at his tremulous confession.

Nathan took a deep breath before meeting Wyatt's stunned gaze head on. "I've never felt like this before. It frightens me a little. I—" He paused and swallowed convulsively. "I don't know if I'll still be myself after—"

Wyatt kissed him then, his mouth tender and hot.

"Stop thinking, Nathan," he murmured against Nathan's lips. "Just feel me. Feel *us*."

He tilted Nathan's chin with a finger and pressed torrid kisses down his throat.

Nathan's heart slammed against his ribs, his senses overwhelmed by Wyatt's love making once more. Heavy pants and gasps left Nathan's mouth as Wyatt touched his body, his strong hands leaving a burning path across Nathan's skin from his shoulders and arms to his chest and belly, his fingers lingering lightly on the scars on Nathan's abdomen and flank.

"*Ah!*" Nathan groaned.

Wyatt had pinched his right nipple between a thumb and forefinger and was tugging and twisting the hard nub.

Nathan arched his back and shuddered.

It wasn't just stings of discomfort he was feeling at Wyatt's rough ministrations.

Every pinch and pull was sending pulses of electricity to his straining cock and his ass.

Wyatt let out a low growl and brought his mouth into play.

"*Oh shit!*" Nathan gasped.

His fingers stabbed Wyatt's hair as the latter closed his hot lips on his left nipple and sucked hard.

"*Aaaah!*"

Nathan squirmed and writhed helplessly in Wyatt's embrace as he repeatedly lavished and tormented his hard nubs with ardent kisses and sucks. He couldn't believe how good Wyatt's mouth felt on his flesh.

He'd had plenty of women play with his nipples before. This was different.

Nathan's eyes rounded when Wyatt closed his teeth on his left nipple and tugged.

A choked cry left his throat at the same time a shot of pre-cum spurted out of his dick and drenched the front of his boxers.

Wyatt let go and glanced down at the damp patch. "Fuck."

He hooked his fingers in the waistband of Nathan's

underwear, kissed Nathan's quivering six-pack and belly, and peeled the material down Nathan's hips and off his legs. Nathan bit his lip when his dick bounced free inches from Wyatt's face, his rock-hard, veiny shaft rosy red and glistening with pre-cum.

A feral expression darkened Wyatt's face as he straightened and raked Nathan's naked body with his gaze.

Nathan shuddered under his hot stare, his ass contracting in a way that brought color to his cheeks and made his heart pound faster. It was as if his body knew where this would eventually end and couldn't wait to be plundered.

Wyatt grabbed Nathan's waist and yanked him toward him, his touch rough.

Nathan gasped and reached up to grab the top of the couch with his hands.

Wyatt's gaze shone a brilliant green as he carefully hooked the back of Nathan's calves on his bare shoulders. He ran his hands up the outside of Nathan's legs, his fingers turning gentle when he reached the scars on Nathan's left thigh. He caressed them with aching tenderness.

"Is this position okay for you?" Wyatt asked huskily.

Nathan took a ragged breath before dipping his chin, his heart melting at Wyatt's loving touch. "Yeah."

"Good." Wyatt fixed Nathan's hips in a powerful grip, leaned down, and flicked the head of Nathan's straining cock with his stiff tongue.

Pleasure sent white spots blazing across Nathan's vision.

"Wyatt!"

Wyatt's hot breath scorched Nathan's aroused flesh. He took his time working Nathan's dick, teasing him with tantalizing licks and flicks of his tongue from the root of his shaft all the way to the tip and back.

Sweet tension coiled inside Nathan's belly. He bucked and writhed in Wyatt's hold, his body straining for release.

I want—shit, I want him to—

Nathan's hands found Wyatt's hair, his touch desperate.

Wyatt met Nathan's wild stare and slowed his taunting movements. His eyes glistened with an untamed light as he allowed Nathan to guide his mouth where he wanted it most.

Wyatt waited, his lips poised above Nathan's straining cock, his heated gaze challenging.

"Tell me what you want, Nathan."

CHAPTER EIGHTEEN

WYATT'S SILKEN COMMAND AND THE FEEL OF HIS
scalding breath on Nathan's sensitive organ almost had
Nathan climaxing there and then. He swallowed,
pressed down on Wyatt's shoulders with his legs, and
curled his fingers in Wyatt's thick locks.

"I want your mouth on me," Nathan mumbled,
unheeding of how wanton he sounded. "I want you to
blow me. I want you to suck my—*aaaah!*"

Heat throbbed through Nathan's lower body as
Wyatt swallowed his flushed dick in one giant gulp.

"*Oh God!*" Nathan gasped. "That feels—*fuck*, that
feels *sooo* good!"

He looked down dazedly and locked eyes with
Wyatt, unable to stop the lustful sounds being ripped
from his throat. The sight of his wet, swollen cock
moving slickly through Wyatt's lips had his entire body
clenching in pleasure.

Wyatt's hands moved to Nathan's butt. He
massaged the taut muscles and bobbed his head

expertly up and down Nathan's rigid shaft, his tongue caressing and flicking Nathan's quivering flesh while he sucked him with strong motions of his jaws.

A buzzing sound filled Nathan's ears, drowning out his gasps and groans. He could feel his orgasm racing down his spine and tightening his balls. He bucked his hips.

A strangled cry escaped him when the movement drove his cock into Wyatt's hot, tight throat.

Wyatt held on to Nathan as he started undulating sensuously off the couch, his heels digging in Wyatt's back, his body under the control of his deepest, most basic instinct.

A fine sheen of perspiration coated Nathan's face as he met Wyatt's dark gaze once more. Harsh grunts left his lungs as he drove his cock repeatedly through Wyatt's lips, fucking Wyatt's mouth with frenzied thrusts of his hips.

Surprise darted through Nathan when Wyatt slipped his fingers inside his crack. He pulled Nathan's buttocks apart, sucked Nathan's dick deep inside his throat, and stroked the pad of a finger gently across his spasming hole.

Nathan came with a hoarse shout, the stimulation sending him over the edge.

He arched his back and convulsed helplessly, his cock pulsing out jet after jet of hot cum inside Wyatt's mouth, his vision swarming with bright sparks of ecstasy.

It felt like forever before Nathan collapsed down on the couch, his pleasantly spent shaft twitching and his belly contracting with aftershocks of pleasure. He was dimly aware of Wyatt letting go of his dick and lowering his trembling legs to the floor.

Nathan blinked hazily when he heard Wyatt's throaty gasp.

He froze at the sight that met his eyes.

Wyatt had freed his erection where he knelt between Nathan's thighs and was giving himself a slow hand job, his hot gaze locked on Nathan's flushed face and his lips parted on heavy breaths.

Air shuddered out of Nathan.

He had never seen anything as carnal as the man pleasuring himself so wickedly before him.

Nathan leaned forward, clasped Wyatt's face, and kissed him hard.

Wyatt groaned, his body tensing even tighter. The sound turned into a curse when Nathan dropped a hand to Wyatt's cock and took over rubbing him.

Nathan shivered as he squeezed and caressed Wyatt's thick, hard length, learning his shape and girth, wondering what it would feel like inside him. His ass contracted at that last thought.

Wyatt's sultry, half-lidded eyes remained focused on Nathan's as they continued kissing and sucking each other's tongues.

Nathan reached down with his other hand and fondled Wyatt's heavy balls.

The way Wyatt's pupils dilated and he hissed told Nathan he loved that move.

Nathan smiled and repeated the teasing motion. He

brought his nails into play and scraped them gently across the hot, rugged sacs.

"*Fuck!*" Wyatt gasped.

He started rolling his hips wildly through Nathan's grip, color staining his cheeks.

Nathan could tell Wyatt was close to coming from his frantic look and ragged pants. He tightened his grip on Wyatt's cock and stroked him faster, his palm slick with Wyatt's pre cum.

He was dying to see Wyatt orgasm again.

A hoarse shout ripped from Wyatt's throat when he climaxed a moment later, his body as rigid as a bow.

Nathan looked down and swallowed heavily as he watched Wyatt explode all over his hand. Wyatt's thick, musky cum seared Nathan's skin and his dick throbbed and pulsed with sweet violence in Nathan's hold as he came. He dropped his head into the crook of Nathan's shoulder, his body shuddering and jerking, his hips pumping his erupting shaft fitfully through Nathan's sticky fingers. His hot breath raised goosebumps on Nathan's flesh where it washed across the side of Nathan's neck.

A sated sigh left Wyatt when he finally stilled some time later. Their pants filled the room as they rested on one another, their hearts thundering against each other's chests.

Wyatt raised his head and looked dazedly at Nathan.

"Wow," he mumbled.

Nathan smiled. "That good, huh?"

"Better than any of my fantasies," Wyatt confessed bluntly.

Nathan flushed.

"Was it good for you too?" Wyatt nibbled Nathan's lower lip with his teeth and caressed Nathan's cock gently.

Nathan groaned, his flesh stirring anew. "Couldn't you tell?"

A sexy smile curved Wyatt's mouth. "I want to hear you say it."

Nathan gasped. Wyatt was stroking his clenching balls. "It was good."

His eyes widened when he noticed Wyatt's growing erection.

How the hell can he be ready to go again so soon?!

Wyatt ignored his dazed stare and arched an eyebrow. "Just good?"

Nathan cursed as Wyatt stroked the head of his stiffening cock lightly with the pad of his thumb.

"Okay, it was spectacular!" he blurted out. "I've never had it so good! Now, about we take a breather—*ah!*"

Wyatt grinned and looked up at Nathan teasingly where he swirled his tongue languorously around Nathan's right nipple.

"Why don't we take this upstairs?"

"You're a beast, you know that?" Nathan groaned.

Wyatt chuckled. "Unfortunately for you, you're *dating* this beast."

He pulled Nathan to his feet and guided him to the staircase and up to his bedroom.

CHAPTER NINETEEN

Wyatt finished making coffee and took his and Nathan's drinks into their office.

"Thanks," Nathan murmured distractedly when Wyatt placed his cup on his desk, his gaze focused on his monitor.

Wyatt hid a smile and crossed the floor to his work station.

He was truly grateful that he and Nathan had managed to keep their personal relationship from intruding on their professional one these past two weeks. He didn't know if it was because they were both guys, or whether it was a result of having been friends before they became lovers.

A contented feeling filled Wyatt at that last word.

Lovers, huh? I never thought I would use that term with regards to Nathan.

Though they were barely halfway into their trial relationship, Wyatt was pleased with how things were going between them. His cock stirred as he thought back to last Sunday. He'd ended up spending the night at Nathan's after they'd made love several times in Nathan's bed. Though they hadn't gone all the way, they'd done plenty to satisfy one another.

Wyatt eyed his desk critically.

Still, it'd be exciting to fool around at the office once in a while. We could totally do it on this table. Or I could sit him in his chair and go down on him.

Wyatt's dick twitched again at that thought. Blowing Nathan was fast becoming one of his favorite activities. He loved how wild Nathan got when he sucked him and his hoarse, untamed grunts as he forcefully shoved his cock inside Wyatt's mouth.

Wyatt studied Nathan where the latter sat concentrating across the way and wondered what it would take to convince him to play out one of his workplace fantasies.

Nathan's cell buzzed next to his hand. Surprise flashed on his face when he glanced at the screen. He took the call.

"Hey, Dean. What's up?"

Dean was Nathan's younger brother. Though they hadn't met, Wyatt had seen a picture of him in Nathan's house. He was a shorter, more slender version of Nathan.

Nathan's eyebrows rose. "You do?" He looked over at Wyatt.

Wyatt frowned faintly at his puzzled expression.

"Sure, I'll check my mail and get back to you." Nathan hesitated. "How's Mom and Dad? They good?"

Relief lightened Nathan's slightly tense expression as he listened to his brother. "That's great."

Wyatt knew Nathan still harbored some lingering guilt when it came to his parents. He'd told Wyatt about his former fiancée and how worried he'd been that breaking off their engagement would jeopardize their parents' friendship and his own relationship with his mother and father.

Confusion lit Nathan's eyes a moment later. "What am I doing two weekends from now?" He glanced at Wyatt. "I usually play poker on Friday. And it's a friend's wedding rehearsal dinner that Saturday." He stiffened. "Wait. You want to visit?"

DREAD SWIRLED THROUGH NATHAN AS HE LISTENED TO Dean. He couldn't explain why he felt uneasy at the thought of his brother coming to Twilight Falls.

Nathan looked over at the man seated across from him.

Is it because I'm not ready to tell him about Wyatt yet?

He frowned faintly.

No. That isn't it. And I'm not ashamed of my relationship with Wyatt.

Still, Nathan knew the news that he was dating a man would come as a shock to his brother.

"Sure," he murmured. "I've got plenty of spare room at my place. Let me know when you're coming."

Nathan ended the call and gazed pensively at his phone.

"Everything okay?" Wyatt said.

Nathan met Wyatt's concerned gaze and berated himself internally. He'd known what he was getting into when he decided to pursue Wyatt. Now was not the time for second thoughts.

"Yeah. Dean said his company has a project for us. And he wants to visit in a couple of weeks." He paused. "I might have to skip our poker game."

"I'm sure the other guys won't mind." Wyatt leaned back in his chair. "Better still, you could bring him along."

Nathan stiffened when he clocked the faint challenge in Wyatt's eyes.

Hang on a minute. Is he testing me?

"That sounds like a great idea," Nathan said, clamping down on his irritation. "By the way, has Izzy said anything to you?"

It was Wyatt's turn to look puzzled. "No. Why?"

"I honestly didn't think she'd last this long," Nathan murmured to himself.

"What do you mean?" Wyatt suddenly froze. His eyes widened. "Wait. Does Izzy know about us?"

Nathan furrowed his brow. "She does, actually."

Wyatt scowled. "Did you tell her?"

"No," Nathan retorted. "Drake did."

Wyatt swore.

Nathan glared. "Why didn't you tell her we were dating?"

Wyatt raked a hand through his hair, his eyes not quite meeting Nathan's. "I just hadn't found the right time," he said, his tone defensive.

Nathan clenched his jaw. "Are you sure that's the only reason?"

Wyatt's expression grew guarded.

Nathan's nails bit into his palms where he'd fisted his hands on his desk.

So, I was right. There was another reason.

"Are you embarrassed about our relationship?" Nathan said coldly.

"No!" Wyatt denied fervently.

Nathan blinked. He knew Wyatt was telling the truth.

"Then why, Wyatt?" he said quietly. "Why don't you want the others to know about us?"

"Because I don't want you to get hurt if this ends badly!" Wyatt blurted out.

Nathan grew deathly still.

"I want you to be able to count Izzy and the guys as your friends even if things don't work out between us," Wyatt mumbled.

A hot feeling stabbed through Nathan's belly. It took a moment to register what it was.

"You've already made up your mind about us, haven't you?" Nathan spat out, unable to mask the pain and anger in his voice. "You are so convinced this relationship will fail you've devised back-up plans." A sudden thought blasted through his mind. Nathan gritted his teeth. "Is it because I haven't gone all the way with you? Is that it, Wyatt?" His tone rose. He knew he was making a scene. But he couldn't stop the words choking his throat. "Is it because we haven't *fucked* in the true sense of the word?!"

Wyatt paled at his bitter recrimination.

"You know that's not true," he whispered. "I don't want to rush you into something you might—"

"Stop!" Nathan snapped. "I've had enough of your excuses!" He rose and headed briskly for the door.

"Where are you going?" Wyatt asked, confused.

"I'm going for a walk. I can't—" Nathan stopped and swallowed as he met Wyatt's pained gaze. "I can't bear to look at you right now!" His heart twisted when he saw the hurt darkening Wyatt's eyes. Wyatt's tortured stare burned Nathan's back as he stormed out of their office.

CHAPTER TWENTY

"What's wrong?"

Elijah handed Nathan a cup of hot chocolate and straddled his work stool, his expression concerned. Nathan clasped the mug gratefully where he leaned against the counter.

His wandering feet had brought him to *La Petite Bouche Gourmande*, where he'd caught Elijah closing up early for the day. The chef had taken one look at Nathan's miserable expression and ushered him inside.

Nathan stared into his drink, his chest painfully tight.

It was the first time he and Wyatt had fought. And it hurt. Badly.

"Is this about Wyatt?"

Elijah's quiet words echoed in the silence that filled the bakery's kitchen.

Nathan raised his chin and met the chef's sedate stare. "You know about us?"

Elijah shrugged. "Only a blind man could fail to see

that Wyatt likes you." He hesitated. "Also, Izzy might have mentioned something about Drake seeing the two of you at *The Watering Hole*."

Nathan swallowed a sigh. "That woman just can't keep a secret, can she?"

"Nope." Elijah smiled faintly. "Still, we all love her for it."

Nathan hesitated before rubbing the back of his head and grimacing ruefully.

"Wyatt and I had a fight."

Elijah stared. "Is it serious?"

Nathan swallowed and nodded.

"If you don't mind me asking, what was it about?" Elijah asked gently.

Nathan gripped his mug hard.

"He doesn't want to tell you guys about us because he thinks we won't last."

Elijah's eyes widened. He pursed his lips. "He told you this?"

Nathan raked his hair with his hand and dipped his chin, suddenly tired.

"I can see why you're upset," Elijah said after a thoughtful pause. "But I can also kinda see Wyatt's point."

Nathan stared.

"He wants to give you a clean way out," Elijah explained in a sympathetic voice. "You've just settled into a new life in Twilight Falls. He doesn't want you to lose the only circle of friends you have in town."

"So, you're saying he's acting with my best interest

in mind?" Nathan was unable to mask the bitterness underscoring his words.

"Something like that," Elijah murmured.

A stilted hush descended on the room.

"Wyatt is scared, Nathan. Just as I was."

Nathan blinked, startled.

Elijah's expression turned oddly serious.

"I didn't want to believe Carter at first, when he told me he was serious about me. I thought he only wanted to sleep with me." He tilted his head and met Nathan's stare head on. "I came to Twilight Falls with a broken heart and a single goal in mind. To open my bakery and make it a success. It took a while for me to see beyond that and be able to trust another man again. To trust Carter." The chef glanced at the titanium band on his left ring finger. He smiled faintly. "I'm so glad I took a chance on him. I can't even imagine my life without Carter and Maisie now. And even if things hadn't worked out between us, I know I would have cherished the time we had together."

Surprise danced through Nathan at Elijah's heartfelt confession. He hadn't realized Carter and Elijah's courtship had been so tumultuous. He rubbed a hand down his face, his frustration rising to the fore again.

"I—I don't know what to do."

"Do you love Wyatt?" Elijah asked.

Nathan stiffened at the chef's candid question. "I care for him. Deeply." He hesitated as he finally faced the truth he had been denying for the past two weeks. "I think I'm more than half in love with him."

Elijah studied him for a silent moment, the look in his eyes strangely shrewd.

"Then you have to make it clear to him. You have to make Wyatt understand that you're committed to making this relationship work. That you are ready to give him your heart, body, and soul."

WYATT PULLED UP OUTSIDE NATHAN'S HOUSE AND turned the SUV's engine off. He stared at the dark building, guilt twisting his stomach. Faint light filtered through the second floor windows.

Nathan's attitude had cooled by the time he'd returned to the office that afternoon. He hadn't addressed the subject of their fight and had left without exchanging more than a handful of words with Wyatt when they'd closed up for the day, his expression aloof.

The words he'd said still echoed in Wyatt's mind.

Wyatt curled his fingers into fists where he grasped the steering wheel.

He knew he'd hurt Nathan. Still, he couldn't curb the incessant voice inside his head that kept telling him that this was too good to be true. That having Nathan care for him as deeply as he did, that having Nathan fall in love with him, was never going to be in the realm of the possible.

Dreams don't just come true. Especially for people like us.

Although Alex and Carter had found the men they wanted to spend the rest of their lives with and their happy-ever-after, there was no guarantee Wyatt, Drake, and Tristan would do the same. Wyatt had come to terms with that cruel reality when he'd gone to Brandon's wedding.

As for Hunter, it was becoming clear something serious was going on between him and his new business rival.

Wyatt steeled himself before stepping out of the car.

I have to apologize to him. I owe him that, at least.

He headed up the path and climbed the porch stairs, his steps resolute.

Nathan opened the door on Wyatt's second knock. His hair was still damp from the shower and he had a towel wrapped around his neck.

His eyes grew guarded as he observed Wyatt. "Come in."

A heavy feeling weighed down on Wyatt as he followed Nathan inside the house and into the kitchen. He could tell Nathan was still furious with him.

Nathan flicked the light switch and crossed the floor to the refrigerator. He got a couple of beers out and handed one to Wyatt.

"Thanks," Wyatt murmured.

Nathan dropped his towel on a chair and wordlessly uncapped his drink. He leaned against the refrigerator and took a swig of his beer, his gaze locked on Wyatt's face. He swallowed slowly before putting the bottle down on the counter next to him with a thunk.

"Why are you here, Wyatt?"

"I'm sorry," Wyatt said quietly. "About what happened today."

Nathan seemed to freeze for a moment. A muscle twitched in his jawline. "Is that it?"

Regret surged through Wyatt at Nathan's shuttered expression.

"No." Wyatt raked his hair with a hand. "I should have told Izzy and the other guys about us. I never intended to make you feel as if I was ashamed of our relationship. You have to believe that."

Nathan frowned. "Is there anything else you want to add to that apology?"

Wyatt blinked. "Hmm, I don't think—" He never got to complete his sentence.

Nathan stormed across the kitchen and grabbed him by the front of his shirt.

"That wasn't what I was angry about Wyatt!" he barked. "I'm upset because, deep down inside, you still don't believe this relationship could work. You don't trust me, Wyatt. That's why you didn't want to tell—"

Wyatt clasped Nathan's face and kissed him, desperate to wipe the tortured look from his beautiful eyes.

Nathan resisted for a moment, his fists twisting in Wyatt's shirt as he tried to push him away. A ragged sound escaped him when he finally surrendered, his mouth opening to welcome Wyatt's demanding tongue, his body shifting closer to Wyatt's frame, as if he were unable to resist his touch.

They kissed deeply, hungrily, passionately, until they had to stop for air. Their pants echoed through the room as they stared at one another, faces flushed and chests heaving.

Wyatt leaned his forehead against Nathan's.

"I'm sorry," he said shakily. "For running scared. For not believing in you."

Nathan gulped, his hands trembling where he pressed them against Wyatt's torso. His eyes had darkened to deep, indigo pools.

Wyatt's heart throbbed with remorse.

I have to be honest with him.

CHAPTER TWENTY-ONE

Wyatt took a deep breath, his eyes full of determination.

"Six months before I met you, I made a promise to myself," he admitted quietly. "That I wouldn't fall in love, ever again."

Nathan blinked, startled by Wyatt's unexpected confession. "What?"

Wyatt wrapped his arms around Nathan and buried his face in Nathan's hair.

"It was at Brandon's wedding."

Shock reverberated through Nathan. "Brandon? As in, *Brandon Taylor?!*"

"Uh huh."

Nathan swallowed as understanding finally dawned. He couldn't help but notice the painful undertone in Wyatt's voice. It made his chest tighten uncomfortably.

"Were you in love with him?" he mumbled.

He could feel Wyatt's thundering heart where their bodies touched.

"I was. You know we went to college together, right?"

Nathan nodded jerkily, his face pressed against Wyatt's shoulder.

"Brandon was my first love. And he's straight."

Nathan's stomach dropped. He finally realized why Wyatt had acted the way he had for the past two weeks.

"I almost didn't go to his wedding," Wyatt murmured. "I mean, why would I want to torture myself, right?"

An ache built inside Nathan at Wyatt's self-deprecating words. He was almost too afraid to ask the question that left him next.

"What made you go in the end?"

Nathan swallowed as he waited for Wyatt's answer.

Is he still in love with Brandon?

Wyatt was quiet for a while.

"I guess I wanted closure," he finally said. "It was the only way I was ever going to be able to get over my unrequited love for him. By seeing him with the woman he'd chosen to spend the rest of his life with."

"Are you a masochist?" Nathan muttered.

A low chuckle rumbled out of Wyatt. "Funny. Izzy said the same thing."

Nathan steeled himself before pulling back and looking at Wyatt.

Elijah's words from that afternoon blazed through his mind.

Elijah's right. I need to make him understand that I'm deadly serious about this.

"I'm not Brandon, Wyatt. I can't do anything about the fact that I've spent most of my adult life having relationships with women." Nathan lifted his hands and cradled Wyatt's stubbled face in a firm hold. "I didn't suggest this trial relationship because I was curious what it would be like to go out with a man." He leaned in and pressed a soft kiss to Wyatt's lips. "I did it because it was *you*, Wyatt. So, I'm begging you. Please don't let me be the only one who wants to give this a real go. I—"

A gasp left Nathan as Wyatt embraced him tightly and kissed him hard. Nathan shuddered and looped his arms around Wyatt's nape.

Wyatt lowered his hands to Nathan's backside and tugged him closer. He finally let go of Nathan's mouth, his hazel eyes bright green and his arms trembling where he held Nathan.

"Do you really mean that?" Wyatt's throat worked convulsively as he gazed into Nathan's eyes.

Nathan nodded jerkily, overcome with emotion.

"God, you kill me," Wyatt breathed. He rubbed his nose tenderly against Nathan's. "I don't know what I did to deserve you."

Nathan smiled tremulously. "Same here."

They gazed at one another, the tension between them slowly melting away, only to be replaced by bewitching desire.

Wyatt shifted uncomfortably and looked down. "What are we going to do about this?"

Nathan's belly clenched as he followed Wyatt's gaze.

They both stared hotly at their straining erections.

"I have a few ideas." Nathan glanced at the table behind him, his heart racing with growing lust.

Wyatt's eyes widened. "Here?"

Nathan arched an eyebrow. "You did say one of your fantasies involved a kitchen table."

Wyatt smiled. "I did say that, didn't I?"

Nathan stepped out of Wyatt's hold. He reached for his T-shirt, shrugged it over his head, and dropped it on the floor. He removed his sweatpants and boxers at a slower pace, Wyatt's hungry gaze following his every teasing move.

"Like what you see?"

Wyatt dipped his chin, his eyes raking Nathan's naked body.

"There's something that'll make it better."

He crossed the floor and removed the apron hanging on a hook by the back door.

"You're kidding?" Nathan mumbled.

"You have no idea how hard it was not to strip you bare but for this apron the last time I was here," Wyatt confessed heatedly.

Nathan flushed when Wyatt hooked the material over his neck and tied the strings around his waist. He shivered as his erect cock grazed the cotton.

Never in a million years could he have imagined that he'd be standing stark naked but for an apron in his kitchen one day, while Wyatt Batista had his wicked way with him.

"What now?" Nathan breathed.

A sinful smile curved Wyatt's mouth. Nathan's pulse rocketed into the stratosphere.

Wyatt took hold of Nathan's waist, backed him to the table, and lifted him so he was sitting on the edge.

Nathan's breathing turned erratic as Wyatt leaned down and took his mouth in a scorching kiss. Wyatt slipped his hands under the apron and stroked Nathan's thighs in soft, seductive motions. Nathan groaned when his erection thickened and tented the material.

Wyatt grinned and started working his way slowly down Nathan's body with his lips, teeth, and tongue, his hot gaze locked on Nathan's.

Nathan's knuckles whitened where he gripped the edge of the table, his heart pounding with excitement.

This was hands down the most erotic thing he had ever done with another human being.

Wyatt lavished Nathan's hard nipples with kisses and sucks through the cotton, making damp patches in the material. He lifted the apron and switched his attention to Nathan's quivering six-pack and stomach, Nathan's exposed, leaking cock inches from his mouth.

A guttural sound punctuated Nathan's ragged pants when Wyatt swirled his tongue teasingly inside his belly button and followed the treasure trail arrowing down to his groin.

By the time Wyatt knelt between Nathan's thighs, Nathan's dick was dripping pre-cum.

Nathan hissed when Wyatt took him boldly into his mouth. He leaned a hand back on the table and curled the other in Wyatt's hair as Wyatt started blowing him slow and deep.

Wyatt's eyes darkened as he worked Nathan's erection, his lips and tongue moving cleverly up and down Nathan's aching shaft. He let go of Nathan's cock, spread his thighs wider, and dipped his head.

"*Aaah!*"

Nathan's toes curled in mid-air when Wyatt sucked his quivering balls into his mouth one at a time, stunned at the electrifying sensation.

Wyatt's breathing grew labored as he moved up and swallowed Nathan's dick once more.

Nathan gasped when he felt his rock-hard organ hit the back of Wyatt's throat.

"Wyatt! I'm gonna—*oh shit*, I'm gonna—*aaah!*"

Wyatt met Nathan's glazed stare as he deep throated him again and again, his fingers biting into Nathan's thighs as Nathan writhed and shuddered on the table, fixing him in place.

Nathan came with a harsh shout, his ears ringing and his entire body stiffening with the intense pleasure of his orgasm. Wyatt gulped and swallowed hungrily as Nathan emptied his hot seed inside his throat, his heavy breaths blowing out of his nose.

Nathan sagged limply when Wyatt released his twitching cock a moment later.

Wyatt maneuvered him onto his feet, turned him around, and bent him over the table, his expression and movements frantic with urgency.

Nathan stiffened, feeling exposed and vulnerable all of a sudden. "Wyatt?"

CHAPTER TWENTY-TWO

"I WANT TO TOUCH YOU," WYATT BREATHED AGAINST Nathan's back. He pressed a hot kiss to Nathan's spine. "Here."

Nathan shuddered when Wyatt caressed his bare butt and stroked a finger down his crack. He hesitated before nodding shakily, anticipation and nerves filling him in equal measures. He'd known this was coming. Still, the raw sensuality of the moment stunned him.

Air shifted behind him.

Nathan shivered when he realized Wyatt was kneeling behind him again.

Wyatt's lips danced lightly across his butt cheeks, raining featherlight kisses on his tense flesh. Heat flooded Nathan's face. His breath locked in his throat in the next instant.

Wyatt had taken hold of his globes and was gently spreading them apart.

Nathan closed his eyes, a little fearful all of a

sudden. He had never felt as defenseless as he did right then, his legs open and his body exposed intimately to another man's stare.

"You're beautiful," Wyatt whispered reverently.

"I really doubt that," Nathan said with a nervous chuckle.

He shuddered when Wyatt circled his hole lightly with the pad of his thumb. Nathan's entrance spasmed and contracted of its own volition, startling him.

"Trust me," Wyatt said fervently. "You have the cutest ass I've ever seen."

Nathan dropped his face in his hands in sheer embarrassment.

"Stop it," he groaned.

A rustle of clothes came from behind him. Nathan looked curiously over his shoulder. His eyes widened.

Wyatt had removed a packet of lube from his wallet and was ripping it open with his teeth.

"Do you always carry that around?" Nathan blurted out.

Wyatt grinned and coated his fingers and palms liberally with the sticky substance.

"Yeah. Ever since we started going out."

He warmed the lube, parted Nathan's crack, and stroked his entrance again.

"Oh!" Nathan sucked in air, his cock twitching.

It felt different with the lube.

Nathan's erection swelled as Wyatt started playing with the tight folds guarding his rear passage, teasing and rubbing them until they gradually softened. He gasped when Wyatt pushed the tip of a finger against his entrance a moment later. To Nathan's amazement, his body gave way and opened up to the intruder.

Nathan bit his lower lip as Wyatt penetrated him with aching tenderness.

"You okay?" Wyatt rasped.

"Yeah." Nathan shivered. "It feels kinda—strange."

"Bear with me," Wyatt said huskily. "It'll feel better soon."

Nathan hissed when Wyatt poured the cool lube directly onto his opening. He flushed as Wyatt began moving his finger in and out of his hole, slowly stretching him, going deeper each time until he was in to the third knuckle.

Wyatt curled his finger inside Nathan's passage and probed around.

A bolt of electricity shot through Nathan when Wyatt pressed against a spot inside him.

"*Aaah!*"

"Found it," Wyatt murmured as Nathan groaned lustily. "That's your prostate, Nathan."

Nathan fisted his hands where he braced his body on the table, staggered by the wicked sensation that had just originated from his back passage. He'd read plenty about anal sex and knew gay men loved nothing more than having their prostate massaged. He just hadn't expected it to feel *that* good.

Wyatt moved his finger in a different angle and repeated the movement.

"*Oh God!*" Nathan shouted, his feet curling on the

floor and his belly tightening with the most insane pleasure.

Wyatt kissed Nathan's left butt cheek and continued working Nathan's sweet spot, his lips hot against Nathan's skin. By the time Wyatt inserted a second finger inside him, Nathan's cock was dripping pre-cum on the floor and his mouth was open on ragged moans and gasps.

A burning sensation built in Nathan's back passage as Wyatt worked the tight band of inner muscles protecting his entrance, spreading him open. He hissed, not sure if he liked the feeling.

Wyatt stopped. "Does it hurt?"

Nathan shuddered and shook his head. He looked over his shoulder and flushed when he met Wyatt's ardent stare. "It stings a little. I can bear it."

Wyatt's face darkened with desire. He rose to his feet and slipped his fingers out of Nathan's body. Nathan swallowed, his passage throbbing at the sudden empty feeling.

Wyatt hurriedly unbuckled his jeans and freed his erection, his movements frantic.

Nathan's eyes widened when Wyatt hooked his left arm around his waist and pulled him in so that Nathan's back was flush against his front. Nathan trembled as Wyatt dipped his hot cock up and down his crack.

An animal sound left Wyatt as he punched his hips and spread his pre-cum along the length of Nathan's cleft. He slipped his left hand under the apron and closed his lubed palm around Nathan's straining erection.

Nathan dropped his head back against Wyatt's shoulder as Wyatt started stroking him, his body taut with tension as his every nerve ending came into play.

Wyatt's heated breath washing across the side of his neck. His strong body supporting Nathan's own quivering one. The proof of his desire rubbing slickly close to Nathan's entrance as he rolled his hips in deep, thrusting motions.

All of it was slowly driving Nathan out of his mind.

A low groan escaped Nathan when Wyatt slipped his right hand between their bodies and sought his twitching hole. Nathan sucked in air and rose on his toes as Wyatt penetrated his softened folds once more, his fingers entering him more easily than he'd imagined they would. The burning discomfort gradually eased as Wyatt stretched his way through the tight ring of inner muscles guarding his back passage.

They both groaned when Wyatt finally lodged his fingers fully inside Nathan's body. Wyatt bit down on Nathan's right earlobe, withdrew his fingers, and thrust them inside again.

"*Fuck!*" Nathan rose on his tip toes, pleasure sending his cock spurting out a jet of hot pre-cum all over Wyatt's hand.

He hooked an arm around Wyatt's neck and braced the other against the table as Wyatt started fucking his cock with his hand and his back passage with his fingers. Harsh grunts left Wyatt as he bucked and punched his own hips against Nathan's butt, his motions so powerful he almost lifted Nathan off the floor.

"Wyatt! *Wyatt!*" Nathan twisted his head around and met the passionate gaze of the man making love to him.

The untamed look on Wyatt's face should have scared him. Yet, Nathan had never felt as cherished as he did in that carnal moment. Wyatt leaned down and took Nathan's mouth in a savage kiss.

Heat pooled deep inside Nathan's belly as Wyatt stroked his cock and plundered the most private part of him with a masterful touch, his fingers massaging and probing Nathan's prostate every time he plunged inside. Nathan gasped as his orgasm danced down his spine and tightened his body like a bow.

Wyatt suddenly clamped his hand around Nathan's throbbing cock.

Nathan moaned in pleasure pain.

"Together," Wyatt growled against Nathan's lips.

Nathan shuddered and gazed into Wyatt's wild eyes as he thrust his rock-hard erection repeatedly through Nathan's crack. Wyatt's pupils dilated as he neared his climax. He started rubbing Nathan's cock again and shoved his fingers harder and faster in and out of Nathan's back passage.

They both shouted hoarsely when they came, their grunts and groans echoing around the kitchen while they made a sticky mess of the floor.

Nathan collapsed onto the table, his body and mind numb with pleasure. He shuddered when Wyatt slumped against his back, his own body twitching with aftershocks of his powerful release, his uneven breaths raising goosebumps on Nathan's nape.

Nathan closed his eyes tight when Wyatt pressed a tender kiss to his hot skin. His heart contracted with a sudden realization.

This is it. This is what I've been waiting for all my life. He is *the one I've been waiting for.*

CHAPTER TWENTY-THREE

"Well, look what the cat dragged in," Izzy said sarcastically where she'd popped her head out of the kitchen. "I barely recognize you, it's been so long."

Wyatt sighed and dropped his keys in the tray on the hallway table.

"We saw each other yesterday morning." He faltered, feeling contrite all of a sudden. "And I know that you know."

Izzy blinked innocently. "I have no idea what you're talking about. I mean, you're my older brother. You'd never lie to me, right? Like, say for example if you started going out with the guy you've had your heart set on for the past three months?"

Another sigh left Wyatt when he detected the edge of steel underscoring her words.

"I didn't lie. I just—I didn't think it was a good idea to announce our relationship to the world when we weren't sure where it was headed."

A thoughtful look came over Izzy. "Does this mean things are getting serious between you two?"

Wyatt made a face and nodded reluctantly.

Izzy pursed her lips. "You want a coffee? I'm making bagels."

Wyatt smiled faintly. This was Izzy's way of waving the proverbial white flag.

"Sure."

He headed into the kitchen and gratefully accepted the drink she poured him.

"I take it from your satisfied expression and the hickey on your neck that you and Nathan patched things up after your fight yesterday?" Izzy said breezily. She buttered a bagel and handed it to him.

Wyatt stiffened as he took the bread roll.

"How did you know Nathan and I had a fight?" he said suspiciously.

Izzy grinned. "My network of spies is exceptionally efficient."

Lines furrowed Wyatt's brow. "Did Elijah tattle?"

"Elijah is an innocent lamb." Izzy sniffed. "And I don't rat on my spies."

Wyatt sighed and bit into his bagel. His body warmed as he relived what had happened between him and Nathan yesterday. He'd ended up spending the night at Nathan's place and they'd gone on to make love another couple of more times before they'd fallen asleep in Nathan's bed.

The mental picture of how Nathan had looked as Wyatt played with his ass was forever etched in his mind. The color staining Nathan's bronzed cheekbones. His dilated pupils and indigo eyes. The way he'd clamped down on his sultry moans as Wyatt stretched his entrance and teased his sweet spot, his hands gripping the headboard and his toes curling in the bedsheet where he lay with his butt propped up on a pillow.

Wyatt couldn't wait to sink his cock in Nathan's virgin hole and fuck him to one screaming orgasm after another.

Izzy narrowed her eyes at him. "You're thinking of something real dirty right now, aren't you?" she said, her tone faintly accusing.

Wyatt blinked and flushed. "I don't know what you mean."

Izzy rolled her eyes hard and took her breakfast to the table. "You do realize how upset the women of Twilight Falls are going to be when they find out you've stolen Nathan from them, don't you?"

"Nathan isn't an object," Wyatt grumbled. "He doesn't belong to anyone."

Izzy gave him a look full of pity. "Wow. You really don't know how the female mind works. And, let's face it, what you really mean is he belongs to *you*." She ignored his guilty expression, slapped a thick layer of cream cheese on her bagel, and pointed the knife at him. "Nathan is the hottest straight man in town right now. Almost every single woman this side of the San Bernardino Mountains is falling over herself trying to get a date with him."

Wyatt gazed warily at Izzy. His stomach knotted with sudden tension.

"Are you—" he faltered. "Umm, are you interested in him too?"

Izzy blinked before bursting out laughing.

"Oh please!" she said between chortles. "I knew the minute I saw the two of you together that you liked him. And he's not my type, nor am I his."

Relief flooded Wyatt. He hadn't realized he'd been holding his breath until he released it in a heavy rush.

"Although, I gotta say, he sure has a hot body," Izzy added with a teasing gleam in her eyes. "And his buns are—" she sucked in air and made slight squeezing motions with her hands, "mighty fine."

Wyatt groaned. Izzy laughed.

She left for work a short while later. Wyatt went to his room and changed clothes. He'd already showered at Nathan's place that morning.

He texted Nathan as he left the house.

Want me to pick you up?

Nathan's reply came almost instantaneously.

I'm already at work.

Wyatt raised an eyebrow. His surprise was replaced by burgeoning unease.

Wait. Does he regret what we did last night?

Wyatt hesitated before tapping out another message.

Everything okay?

This time, Nathan's reply took longer to come through.

I need to prepare myself.

Wyatt frowned.

Why?

I don't know how to face you. I mean, you were playing with my ass only hours ago.

A snort escaped Wyatt. He grinned.

I wouldn't have put you down as the shy type.

I'm not. But you were inside me. Thoroughly. Your fingers are the work of the devil.

Wyatt chuckled. He could totally imagine Nathan's flushed face right now.

And your ass was amazing.

Stooop!

Like, totally phenomenal. I can't wait to taste it.

A horrified emoji popped up on Wyatt's cell. He laughed out loud.

Wait! You mean you wanna put your mouth down...

Yeah.

Like, kiss it and stuff?

Lick it, kiss it, rim it. Poke inside and play around with my tongue. You're gonna love it.

Three horrified emojis blasted across Wyatt's screen, followed by an ellipsis. His cell buzzed with another incoming message.

...Okay...

Wyatt swallowed a groan.

He's going to be the death of me.

CHAPTER TWENTY-FOUR

"Happy Birthday, Wyatt!"

Nathan grinned as colorful poppers exploded all over the man wearing a cone party hat and a somewhat aggravated expression where he sat at the head of the table.

It was the night of Wyatt's birthday and the whole gang had gathered at Wyatt and Izzy's place. Since Wyatt had been adamant he didn't want a big outside affair, Izzy had organized a cozy celebratory dinner with just their close friends.

"I really am too old for this," Wyatt grumbled to his sister when she brought out the cake Elijah had baked specially for the occasion.

"You're right," she said, tongue in cheek. "I can't possibly fit all thirty-one candles on top of this thing. Oh, thanks, sweetie."

Maisie handed Izzy the pretty wax sticks Elijah had brought along to decorate the cake. The little girl scurried over to Carter, tugged the cuff of his shirt sleeve until he bent down, and whispered in his ear.

"Yes, you can, honey." Carter kissed the top of her head.

Maisie beamed and disappeared from the kitchen. She returned a minute later with a carefully wrapped package.

"Here's your present, Uncle Wyatt," the little girl said shyly as she handed it to Wyatt.

"Thank you, sweetheart," Wyatt said with a smile.

Nathan's heart flip-flopped as he watched the two of them together.

He'll make a great father.

Nathan knew this thing between him and Wyatt was getting serious fast. Instead of alarming him, he found himself strangely content with the situation. They were great friends, excellent business partners, had fantastic chemistry in the bedroom, and respected and admired each other deeply.

Wyatt was perfect for him in every sense of the word and Nathan couldn't think of a single reason why they shouldn't turn their trial relationship into the real deal.

It was a subject he intended to address tonight and one he hoped he and Wyatt shared the same opinion on.

"Looks like things are going well for you two," Drake said where he sat beside Nathan.

"They are."

Drake arched an eyebrow. "So, you don't have any regrets?"

Nathan shrugged. "None."

Elijah smiled across the way.

"I still can't believe Finn and I were the last ones to find out you and Wyatt were dating," Alex grumbled.

His husband sighed next to him. "We didn't exactly shout it from the rooftops when we started, you know —" Finn waggled his eyebrows suggestively.

Alex flushed. "This and that are different."

"I really wish you guys would stop talking about sex in front of Maisie," Tristan muttered.

"What's 'sex,' Uncle Tristan?" Maisie piped up in an innocent voice behind him.

Carter frowned. Elijah chuckled.

It was midnight by the time the party ended. Nathan stayed back and helped Izzy and Wyatt clear up.

"Don't stay up too late you two," Izzy said after they'd finished. She yawned and waved a hand at them over her shoulder as she headed for the stairs.

Wyatt linked his fingers with Nathan's when she disappeared from view.

"Thank you for my present. I love it."

He raised Nathan's hand and pressed a kiss to his knuckles, his eyes bright and the watch Nathan had given him gleaming prettily on his wrist.

Nathan's pulse fluttered when the air between them slowly thickened with sexual tension.

"You're welcome."

Wyatt pulled Nathan close and looped his arms around his waist. "You're spending the night here, right?" He nudged Nathan's nose gently with his own.

Nathan dipped his chin, feeling inexplicably shy all of a sudden. It was the first time he would be staying over at Wyatt's place as his lover.

"I have an overnight bag in the car." He hesitated before glancing in the direction of the stairs.

"Don't worry." Wyatt pressed a light kiss to his lips. "Izzy's room is at the other end of the house."

A bout of nervousness shot through Nathan then. "Let me get my bag."

He slipped out of Wyatt's arms without meeting his eyes and headed down the hall to the entrance. A cool breeze danced across his hot skin when he stepped out on the porch.

Nathan took a shaky breath and walked over to his car.

Damn. I didn't think I'd be so skittish.

By the time he returned to the house, Nathan had a better handle on his nerves.

Wyatt was waiting for him in the hall. Nathan registered his aloof expression with a jolt of surprise. Wyatt wordlessly took the bag from his hand, dropped it on the floor, and crouched in front of him.

Nathan gasped as Wyatt hooked his arms around the back of his thighs, hoisted him effortlessly over his shoulder, and straightened to his full height.

"What the—?!"

"I can't help but feel you might bolt at any second," Wyatt said gruffly. "I don't know what's going on inside your head tonight, but we're going to talk about it in my room."

Nathan groaned as Wyatt carried him to the stairs.

"This is so embarrassing," he mumbled against Wyatt's back.

"It's your own fault," Wyatt said, unrepentant. He turned left at the top of the staircase and headed down a dimly lit corridor to a room at the far end.

Nathan had an impression of gray walls and gauzy curtains fluttering at dual aspect windows before he was dropped unceremoniously on his back on the king size bed dominating the floor.

Wyatt closed the door, switched the light on, and approached the bed with a predatory look on his face.

Nathan swallowed and sat up. *Oh boy.*

"Are you having second thoughts about us?"

Nathan blinked at Wyatt's stilted question. "No."

Wyatt leaned over him and braced his arms on either side of his body, trapping him in.

"Then what?" he murmured inches from Nathan's lips.

"I think we should end our trial relationship," Nathan blurted out.

Wyatt froze.

Nathan cursed. "I mean, I think we should turn it into, you know—" He stopped and chewed his lower lip, mortification bringing a flood of color to his face.

Wyatt stared. His stiff expression slowly cleared. "You mean, you want us to have a real relationship?"

Nathan's heart twisted at the hope underscoring Wyatt's voice. He couldn't stop from reaching out to him then. He clasped Wyatt's face in his hands and stole a sweet kiss from his lips.

"Yes. I want the real deal. All of it." Nathan pressed

his forehead against Wyatt's. "Do you know what I thought when I saw you with Maisie tonight?"

Wyatt shook his head, his cheeks slightly flushed.

"I thought you'd make a great father one day." Nathan kissed Wyatt again. "And I want to be the one standing beside you when that happens."

Wyatt's eyes widened. "Do you—" He stopped and swallowed. "Do you mean that?!"

"Yes," Nathan breathed against his lips.

Wyatt smiled tremulously. "I'm not gonna let you sleep tonight, you know that, right?"

Nathan grinned. "I'm prepared for that." He let go of Wyatt and flopped down on the bed, his arms spread wide. "Take me, oh master."

Wyatt laughed at his solemn command. "You might live to regret those words."

Nathan shook his head, his heart swelling with happiness all over again as he met Wyatt's heated gaze. "I don't have any regrets. About you. About us. About this. Make me yours, Wyatt."

CHAPTER TWENTY-FIVE

Wyatt's chest contracted with dizzying joy at the dazzling look in Nathan's eyes.

He'd hoped and prayed that he and Nathan would go all the way tonight. What he hadn't expected was Nathan's heartfelt confession just now, or his aspirations for their future.

It was clear Nathan had given their relationship a great deal of thought.

Wyatt almost wanted to pinch himself, so stunned was he about the night's developments. He promised himself then that he would always cherish this man. That he would do his utmost to make him happy or die trying.

Wyatt removed Nathan's shoes and dropped them on the floor.

They landed heavily on the wooden boards, the only sound in the room bar their accelerating breathing.

Nathan inhaled sharply when Wyatt raised his left

foot and sucked his big toe into his mouth. The color staining Nathan's cheekbones and the way his cock swelled behind the zipper of his jeans told Wyatt he loved that move.

Nathan reached up and undid Wyatt's belt buckle, his expression feverish.

They undressed each other rapidly, hands trembling and chests heaving.

Wyatt raked Nathan's naked form with his hungry gaze as he pushed him back down on the bed.

He had never seen anyone as beautiful as the man he was about to make love to.

He removed a new bottle of lube and a box of condoms from the nightstand and dropped them on the bed. Nathan panted as Wyatt climbed onto the mattress and crowded him onto the sheet. A groan left his lips when their bodies kissed from their chests all the way to their groins.

Nathan looped his arms around Wyatt's nape and opened his mouth eagerly under Wyatt's hungry kiss, his dick throbbing against Wyatt's thigh.

Wyatt melded their tongues together, probing and learning every inch of Nathan's mouth all over again. He wanted to mark Nathan tonight. To brand him with his lips and his fingers and his cock. To make it so that he would never experience such dizzying pleasure with another person but him.

It was a selfish wish. But Wyatt wanted it nonetheless.

He let go of Nathan's lips and rained scalding kisses down his neck.

"You're driving me crazy!" Nathan groaned.

Nathan's tortured voice had blood surging to Wyatt's groin. He sucked and kissed the pulse thrumming furiously at the base of Nathan's throat and stroked Nathan's arms and shoulders with featherlight caresses.

"Aaah!"

Nathan gasped and arched his back when Wyatt pinched and tugged his nipples.

Wyatt growled and shifted down the bed. He alternated between kneading Nathan's hard nubs between his forefinger and thumb, and circling and flicking them with the stiff tip of his furrowed tongue.

Nathan hissed with every pull and twist, his cock pulsing musky pre-cum against Wyatt's leg.

Wyatt worked Nathan's swollen nubs with his hands and sucked and licked his way down Nathan's shuddering six-pack. He kissed the fine scars adorning Nathan's body with scorching tenderness before arrowing in on Nathan's groin.

Nathan propped himself up on his elbows when Wyatt parted his thighs and settled between them. Wyatt held Nathan's passion glazed gaze, hooked Nathan's knees over his shoulders, and went to town on Nathan's trembling dick.

"Wyatt! *Oh God!*"

Nathan dropped back on the bed and curled his fingers punishingly in Wyatt's hair as Wyatt bobbed his head up and down his hard length, taking him deep. His groans and gasps resonated hotly in Wyatt's ears as

Wyatt held on to his thighs and blew him rapidly toward an orgasm.

Wyatt grunted when Nathan exploded at the back of his throat a moment later. He swallowed Nathan's hot cum hungrily and milked his pulsing cock to the last drop with gentle sucks and licks.

Nathan moaned when Wyatt released his spent shaft with a wet pop and moved his legs back down on the bed.

"Thank you for dessert." Wyatt smiled and flicked Nathan's quivering balls with his tongue where he lay in the cradle of his thighs.

Nathan hissed and shuddered. He lay trembling and panting for a moment before sitting up, his expression determined.

Wyatt's eyes widened when Nathan tugged him up onto his knees.

"I want to do the same to you."

Wyatt's erection twitched at Nathan's words.

LOOKS LIKE HE LIKES THAT IDEA, HUH?

Nathan's pulse raced as he grazed Wyatt's rock-hard shaft with a knuckle.

"Is that okay, Wyatt?" He settled down on the bed, looked up at Wyatt from under his lashes, and grasped his thick, hot length with one hand. "Can I blow you?"

"*Fuck!*" Wyatt made a strangled sound and bucked his hips as Nathan started rubbing him.

Nathan smiled. "I'm going to take that as a yes."

Wyatt groaned and fisted his hands on Nathan's shoulders when Nathan brought his mouth into play. Nathan's belly clenched as he swirled his tongue on the rosy head of Wyatt's erection.

He'd never given head to a man before, but he'd been at the receiving end of plenty and knew what he needed to do. Wyatt's grunts and increasingly heavy breathing told Nathan that he loved what he was doing to him.

He stroked Wyatt's cock with brisk, twisting motions of his fingers and licked his shaft from the root all the way to the top and back.

"Shit!" Wyatt gasped. "That feels good!"

Nathan's own dick twitched at the pleasure darkening Wyatt's eyes.

He explored the thick veins covering Wyatt's length with his lips, teased his heavy balls with his tongue, and played with the leaking tip with his thumb.

Wyatt's hands found Nathan's head. "Nathan."

Nathan inhaled through his nose, grasped Wyatt's thighs, and finally took his cock inside his mouth like he so desperately wanted him to.

"Oh!" Wyatt groaned and jerked his hips.

Nathan concentrated on controlling his breathing as he slowly worked Wyatt's cock with his lips and tongue. Wyatt's thick length bulged his cheeks and the scent and taste of his cum filled his nostrils and mouth. He bobbed his head to and fro and carefully swallowed him deeper.

A guttural noise erupted from Wyatt when the tip of his cock stroked the back of Nathan's throat. Nathan met Wyatt's glazed stare, sucked Wyatt's cock out of his mouth, and took him back in with a sultry motion.

Wyatt swore and twisted his fingers in Nathan's hair. He finally succumbed to his body's instincts and started rolling and punching his hips.

Nathan's erection swelled and thickened as Wyatt fixed his head in place and fucked his mouth with increasing urgency.

He never would have imagined giving head to a man would be so exciting.

The silky feel of Wyatt's hot, turgid shaft filling his mouth to the brim. The coarse roughness of his trimmed pubes where they tickled Nathan's lips. His salty cum coating Nathan's tongue liberally with the evidence of his arousal.

All of it was unbelievably titillating.

Nathan dropped a hand to his cock and started stroking himself as he blew Wyatt deeper and faster toward a climax.

Wyatt came with a hoarse shout, his grip punishing where he held Nathan's head. Nathan panted through his nose and gulped Wyatt's sticky seed as it pulsed against the back of his throat, his own dick throbbing out his arousal.

Wyatt shuddered and gently removed his spent dick from Nathan's mouth. He tugged Nathan up onto his knees and took his lips in a savage kiss.

"You do know where my mouth has just been, right?" Nathan mumbled when Wyatt released his lips.

Wyatt smiled. "I do. Now, how about we start round two?"

CHAPTER TWENTY-SIX

Nathan gasped when Wyatt turned him to face the headboard and maneuvered him onto his hands and knees.

"Wyatt?"

Wyatt opened the nightstand drawer and took something out.

Nathan's eyes widened when he saw the red silk scarf in Wyatt's hand. The memory of the night he'd forced Wyatt to confess his feelings for him stormed through his mind.

Heat flooded Nathan's face and his belly clenched with anticipation.

"Remember this?" Wyatt asked huskily.

Nathan nodded, his heart pounding with excitement. He shuddered when Wyatt gently blindfolded him.

"Are you scared?"

Nathan swallowed and shook his head at Wyatt's question.

"No," he breathed. "Nothing you do to me would ever scare me."

He shivered when he felt Wyatt's mouth graze his nape.

"Good. This will make you…feel things more."

Wyatt pressed a hot kiss to Nathan's skin and skimmed Nathan's spine with his lips.

Nathan squeezed the sheet with his hands when the mattress dipped behind him.

He knew Wyatt was crouched behind him. And he realized what Wyatt intended to do next.

"*Oh!*" Nathan sucked in air when Wyatt nipped his left butt cheek with his teeth.

Wyatt soothed the love bite with a tender kiss before doing it all over again.

By the time Wyatt spread Nathan's cleft open and exposed his hole, Nathan was trembling with arousal and his cock was dripping onto the bed.

The first flick of Wyatt's tongue against his entrance ripped a guttural shout from his throat.

"*Oh God!*"

Nathan reached out blindly and grasped the headboard with one hand, the illicit sensation so wicked he could hardly wait for what came next.

Wyatt obliged him by repeatedly teasing his tight pucker with his furrowed tongue, causing his opening to twitch and contract. Stars exploded across Nathan's red-tinged vision when Wyatt brought his lips into play and kissed and sucked his folds. Nathan dropped his head and moaned and keened and gasped as Wyatt relentlessly tortured his virgin entrance, getting him ready for what was still to come.

His softened hole gradually relaxed and opened under Wyatt's ardent ministrations.

"*Aaah!*" Nathan's cock jerked out a jet of cum when Wyatt spread him open with thumbs and penetrated him with his tongue.

Nathan lost all sense of time as Wyatt plundered his opening with his tongue, going deeper with every stab of his stiff flesh, rimming him thoroughly. Sweet tension tightened his belly as his orgasm built in savage waves. He started thrusting his hips, powerless to resist his body's base instincts.

Nathan braced a hand against the headboard and moved to and fro, Wyatt following his movements with his tongue. He reached down toward his aching cock.

Wyatt's fingers found Nathan's erection before he did. He closed his palm around Nathan's quivering shaft and started stroking him briskly.

Hot pulses of pleasure throbbed through Nathan as Wyatt rimmed and rubbed him toward his climax. Sweat dripped down his forehead and soaked into the silk scarf as he opened his mouth on rising gasps and grunts.

A buzzing sound filled Nathan's ears. He fisted his hands, arched his head and spine, and came with a long, low cry. The orgasm stormed violently through his body, wreaking havoc on his senses, causing his world to spin with sweet ferocity. White light pulsed across his vision in tandem with his jerking cock as he convulsed and undulated on the mattress, the bed creaking beneath his savage motions.

It felt like a lifetime before awareness finally returned. Nathan felt Wyatt undo the scarf. He blinked, his heart still thundering in his throat and his belly and thighs trembling and aching with the force of his climax.

Wyatt hooked an arm around Nathan's waist and sat back, taking Nathan's limp body with him. He kissed Nathan's right ear tenderly.

"You okay?"

Nathan nodded shakily, still too breathless to speak.

He could feel Wyatt's steely length against his butt.

"That was—*wow*," he finally mumbled.

Wyatt chuckled. "That good, huh?"

"I thought I was going to pass out," Nathan confessed.

Wyatt's laughter rumbled against Nathan's back. It turned into a groan when Nathan tentatively wiggled his backside against Wyatt's staining erection.

"We still need to take care of that."

"I don't want to hurt you."

Nathan looked at him over his shoulder. "You won't. I mean, if your fingers and tongue made me come so hard I almost lost consciousness, I bet your dick will send me into outer space."

Wyatt chuckled. He kissed Nathan and reached down to rub Nathan's cock.

It wasn't until Nathan was breathing heavily and his erection was at full mast once more that Wyatt guided him onto his hands and knees again.

"Your first time will be easier from behind," Wyatt explained at Nathan's expression.

Nathan pursed his lips. "But I won't see your 'O' face."

Wyatt groaned. "We'll do it missionary style next."

"Promise?"

Wyatt took his mouth in a passionate kiss. "I'm gonna do you in every position that exists tonight."

Nathan shivered at the desire burning in his green eyes.

Wyatt opened the bottle of lube, warmed a generous amount of the stuff in his palms, and brought his fingers to Nathan's butt.

Nathan's dick throbbed as Wyatt played with his entrance before slowly thrusting two fingers inside him. His passage burned and stung when Wyatt scissored his fingers and stretched the inner band of muscles inside him, working the stiff ring open.

A hiss left his lips when Wyatt slowly inserted a third finger inside him.

Wyatt kissed his trembling back. "Does it hurt a lot?"

Nathan bit his lip. "I can bear it."

Wyatt reached around Nathan's hips and started rubbing his cock.

The stimulation distracted Nathan from the discomfort in his back passage. The pain gradually eased. A sweet ache replaced it.

His body felt empty, as if it needed something to fill it up.

Bolts of pleasure danced through Nathan as Wyatt's

fingers bumped lightly against his prostate, his thrusting motion slick from the lube.

"Wyatt?" Nathan whispered.

"Yes?"

"I—I think I'm ready."

Wyatt slowed his hand. His breath shuddered out of him as he removed his fingers from Nathan's body. Nathan saw him reach for a condom out of the corner of his eyes and fisted his hands in the bedsheet, his pulse thumping in anticipation.

He heard the rip of the foil and Wyatt's heavy pants as he sheathed himself.

Nathan looked over his shoulder and met Wyatt's feverish gaze as the latter crowded his back and took hold of his butt. Their eyes stayed locked as Wyatt parted his cleft and brought his thick cock to Nathan's opening.

CHAPTER TWENTY-SEVEN

WYATT PUSHED INSIDE WITH SLOW, GENTLE THRUSTS OF his hips, his cheeks flushed and his pupils dilated. Nathan bit his lip, dropped his head forward, and relaxed his body, willing it to accept the man entering him.

His hole tingled as it was stretched wide by Wyatt's erection. Nathan closed his eyes as Wyatt slowly filled him, stunned by the new feeling. He gasped and gritted his teeth when Wyatt's cock pushed against the tight ring inside him, the burning sensation returning ten-fold.

"Breathe through your mouth," Wyatt ordered.

Nathan did as Wyatt instructed and panted through his open lips. The pain gradually eased. Nathan moaned, the hungry feeling he'd experienced before sweeping over his body again.

Wyatt's fingers clenched on Nathan's hips. He pulled out and thrust back inside.

Sparks exploded across Nathan's vision as the

sudden motion seated Wyatt fully inside him.

Wyatt stilled, giving Nathan time to adjust to the penetration.

Nathan licked his lips and tentatively squeezed the thick intruder filling his passage.

The movement elicited gasps of pleasure from both of them.

"You're so big," Nathan mumbled.

Wyatt's body shook as he groaned and chuckled.

"In any other circumstance but this one, I would take that as a compliment."

Nathan fisted his hands in the bedsheet and rocked his hips slightly.

The motion drew another throaty gasp from him and a lusty groan from Wyatt.

"What I mean is, it feels good. We're a perfect fit."

"*Shit!* You're driving me crazy!" Wyatt hissed. "You don't know how badly I want to pound your ass with my cock right now!"

Nathan glanced at him over his shoulder, his heart thudding and his stomach knotting with eager anticipation.

"What's stopping you?"

An animal sound left Wyatt. He grasped Nathan's hips in a punishing grip, pulled out, and pushed back inside with a powerful thrust.

Nathan gasped and arched his back, stunned by the savage sensation of being taken. Pleasure mixed with burning pain as Wyatt started fucking him the way he'd always wanted to. Hard and fast. Slow and deep.

The pain soon faded and all that was left was

dizzying pleasure and the most fulfilling feeling of intimacy Nathan had ever experienced during the act of love making.

It was when Wyatt pulled Nathan's hips high and rose on his feet to fuck him in a crouched position that things got wild.

"Aaah! Oooh!"

Nathan moaned and gasped as the new position caused Wyatt's rock-hard cock to massage and probe his prostate with every forceful thrust of his body. He braced his hands against the headboard and jerked and rolled his own hips backward with equal strength, meeting Wyatt's deep penetration.

The most exquisite tension wound through Nathan as they mated with untamed passion, the bed groaning and squeaking under their dancing bodies.

His first orgasm hit him like a freight train.

A choked cry left Nathan as he shuddered and convulsed, his dick and ass throbbing and pulsing with violent waves of pleasure. Wyatt grunted as the motion squeezed and milked his cock where he plundered Nathan's passage.

Shock bolted through Nathan as he shuddered and trembled in the aftermath of his climax. His dick was still erect.

Wyatt bit down on Nathan's right earlobe and tugged. "Good," he growled. "You're still hard."

Nathan gasped when Wyatt suddenly pulled out of his body. Air left his lungs in a heavy whoosh as Wyatt flipped him on his back. Wyatt yanked a pillow under

Nathan's butt, settled between his thighs, and propped his calves on his shoulders.

"Now you can see my 'O' face," Wyatt said with a sultry grin as he brought his rigid cock to Nathan's entrance once more.

He spread Nathan's twitching hole with his thumbs and plunged inside him with a deep, powerful thrust.

Pleasure throbbed through Nathan's back passage as Wyatt filled him to the brim again and again. He grasped the headboard with his hands and met Wyatt's rolling hips with eager jerks of his own pelvis, his breaths shuddering out of him, his eyes locked on Wyatt's lustful expression.

He had never made love as sensually and as savagely as he was doing right now.

And every thrust of Wyatt's body, every grunt and gasp of pleasure that ripped from his throat, every painful clench of his fingers on Nathan's hips, told him it was the same for Wyatt.

Nathan's belly clenched when the first wave of his orgasm swirled through him once more. His balls tightened and rose and his nipples ached as he neared the crest, his knuckles whitening on the headboard above him.

Wyatt's dilated pupils and ragged breathing told Nathan he was close to exploding too.

They climaxed together, their mouths open on low keens of ecstasy, the bed shuddering with their rocking motions. Wyatt leaned down and took Nathan's mouth in a scorching kiss as he pumped his hips fitfully against his ass, his cock swelling and pulsing out cum inside the condom while Nathan came all over their chests.

It wasn't until they both stilled that Wyatt hooked Nathan's legs around his waist and collapsed onto him, sweat dripping off his nose.

Nathan embraced Wyatt tightly while he gasped and panted against his shoulder, his mind still blank and his body trembling with aftershocks of pleasure. He let out a low protest when Wyatt gently pulled out of him.

Wyatt disposed of the condom and returned to Nathan's arms.

"You okay?" He kissed Nathan tenderly and moved his hand down Nathan's body.

Nathan shivered when Wyatt stroked the softened folds of his entrance with a finger.

"Yeah." He swallowed. "That was even more amazing."

Wyatt smiled. "I'm flattered that Twilight Falls' lady killer thinks I'm great at sex."

Nathan narrowed his eyes slightly. "I thought we dropped that topic a while back. And you're still on probation."

Wyatt arched an eyebrow. "How?"

Nathan folded his hands behind his head. "If I recall correctly, you promised to fuck me until dawn. In *every* position."

Wyatt sighed. "You won't be able to walk tomorrow if I really do that."

"It's Sunday. You can give me a hot bath and a massage."

Wyatt groaned when Nathan pushed him onto his back and wriggled down his body until he was face to face with his cock.

"I forgot part of that reputation of yours alluded to your stamina." Wyatt's grumble turned into a hiss.

Nathan had closed a hand around his shaft and was stroking and kissing his dick with eager enthusiasm.

"Yup. Now, shut up and let me blow you."

CHAPTER TWENTY-EIGHT

Wyatt winced when the stairs creaked under his feet. He eyed Nathan's overnight bag where it sat by the front door and glanced over his shoulder in the direction of Izzy's bedroom.

Maybe she's not up yet.

He knew leaving the bag there would only invite a whole host of questions from his nosy sister. He'd just reached the bottom of the stairs when Izzy's voice rose behind him.

"What are you doing up so early? I thought for sure you'd have stayed in bed today."

"I, er, wanted a coffee," Wyatt mumbled.

Izzy's expression turned suspicious. Her gaze shifted past Wyatt's shoulder. It widened slightly when it landed on Nathan's overnight bag. A smile curved her lips. She cast a shrewd look in the direction of Wyatt's bedroom.

"I see."

To Wyatt's surprise, she strolled past him and headed in the direction of the kitchen.

"That's it?" Wyatt blurted out.

Izzy stopped and looked over her shoulder. "What?"

"I thought I was gonna have to go through the Spanish Inquisition this morning," Wyatt said suspiciously.

Izzy sighed. "Oh, come on. I *can* be tactful, you know."

"Since when?" Wyatt said.

Izzy frowned. "Don't poke the bear, Wyatt."

Wyatt blew out a sigh and retrieved Nathan's bag. He had his foot on the bottom step when Izzy reappeared, a glass of water and some pills in hand.

"Here." She offered them to Wyatt.

"What's this?"

"Painkillers." Izzy's eyes sparkled as she grinned. "You know, for the guy you deflowered last night. I bet his ass is on—"

The rest of her words were drowned out by Wyatt's groan as he headed up the stairs.

Nathan was still fast asleep when he entered his bedroom. His dark hair was all tousled where he lay on his front, lips parted on soft breaths and the bedsheet riding low on his hips.

Desire stirred inside Wyatt as he raked the smooth line of Nathan's back and the sweet curve of his butt. The hickeys and love bites he'd made on Nathan's body were gloriously evident against his honey colored skin.

Wyatt carefully placed Nathan's bag on a chair, put the water and pills on the nightstand, and sat on the edge of the bed. He reached out and touched Nathan's slightly swollen lips with light fingers.

His groin tightened as he recalled where Nathan's mouth had been just a few hours ago.

There was no doubt in Wyatt's mind that last night had been the best night of his entire adult life. He had never known such passion before, nor had he ever made love as hungrily as he had done to Nathan.

He would never get enough of Nathan. Wyatt was certain of this now.

Nathan's eyes fluttered open.

"Sorry." Wyatt lowered his hand to the bed. "I didn't mean to wake you."

Nathan blinked fuzzily. His expression slowly cleared.

He reached for Wyatt's fingers, the warm look in his eyes making Wyatt's heart flutter all over again.

"Hey." Nathan started moving onto his side and suddenly blanched. "Oh!"

His fingers clenched tightly on Wyatt's hand and he bit down hard on his lip.

Guilt stormed through Wyatt as Nathan carefully rolled back onto his front and buried his face in the pillow.

"Are you okay?" Wyatt asked anxiously.

"Give me a minute," Nathan mumbled. He winced and swallowed. "Shit. I did not think it would hurt this bad."

Wyatt leaned over and kissed Nathan's back, his stomach twisting with fresh remorse.

"I'm sorry. I'll draw you a bath right now."

He went into the bathroom, turned the taps on the ornate clawfoot tub dominating the space, and threw a generous amount of Epsom salt in the steaming water.

He knew he'd been too rough with Nathan last night, considering it was Nathan's first time experiencing penetrative sex. He should have held back, despite Nathan's pleas to the contrary.

I'm such an asshole.

Nathan's face had regained some color by the time Wyatt returned to the bedroom. He groaned when Wyatt carefully scooped him up in his arms and carried him into the bathroom. A soft sigh left him when Wyatt lowered him into the tub.

"That feels good," Nathan breathed as he sank into the water.

Wyatt retrieved the painkillers and water from the nightstand and made Nathan swallow the pills.

"Will you stop looking at me as if you've committed some unforgivable sin?" Nathan said wryly after he'd taken the medicine. "I'm at fault too."

"I'm more experienced at this," Wyatt said, contrite. "I should have stopped after the first round."

Nathan narrowed his eyes. "That would have left me sorely disappointed."

"Well, now, you're just sore."

Nathan blinked before bursting out laughing. His chuckle morphed into a grimace. "Youch. Even laughing hurts."

"I'm sorry," Wyatt said in a morose voice.

Nathan sighed. "Stop apologizing." A thoughtful look dawned on his face. "Actually, if you're really sorry, you should do something to compensate me." He eyed the bathtub with a calculating expression. "This thing looks big enough for both of us."

Wyatt stared. "I think that's a bad idea."

Nathan's expression turned wolfish. "And I think it's a great idea. Don't worry. I'm not letting you anywhere near my ass for at least a week." He grinned at Wyatt's downcast look, folded his arms on the edge of the clawfoot tub, and propped his chin atop them. "Now, how about you strip and get in here?"

Wyatt's pulse accelerated at the passionate light in Nathan's eyes. He rose, unzipped his jeans, and kicked them off his legs.

Nathan's gaze arrowed in on Wyatt's swelling erection.

"Man, I can't believe *that* was inside me."

Wyatt swallowed at Nathan's husky words.

He's driving me out of my mind.

"Move over."

Nathan shuffled forward at Wyatt's command.

Wyatt climbed in behind him, squatted, and carefully stretched his legs out on either side of Nathan's body.

Nathan leaned his back against Wyatt's chest.

"This is bliss," he murmured.

Wyatt had to agree.

The feel of Nathan's body against his own. Nathan's hair tickling his chin. The hot water caressing their bodies intimately.

All of it felt heavenly.

Steam swirled around them as they rested against one another, the silence between them comfortable.

"I did promise you a massage," Wyatt said after a while.

"You did?"

"Uh huh." Wyatt raised his hands and started rubbing Nathan's shoulders in slow, deep motions.

"*Hmm*," Nathan hummed in pleasure.

Wyatt's cock twitched at the sound.

"Is it me or is your dick getting harder?" Nathan said wryly after a minute.

"I can't help it," Wyatt groaned as he kneaded Nathan's back. "You keep making erotic noises."

"They are hums of appreciation," Nathan protested.

Wyatt kissed his nape. "Everything you do is erotic."

Nathan shot Wyatt a hot look over his shoulder.

"I did say you were going nowhere near my ass, right? That statement still stands."

"I'm not going to enter you," Wyatt promised. "But, there's plenty of other things I can do to pleasure you."

Nathan's glazed over slightly. "Maybe this was a bad idea after all."

Wyatt kissed Nathan and dropped his hands to Nathan's hips. "No, it was a great idea."

By the time he finished massaging Nathan's shoulders, back, and legs, Nathan's twitching cock was at full mast. Wyatt licked his lips as he eyed Nathan's flushed dick through the water's surface.

"Wyatt," Nathan panted. He dug his fingers into Wyatt's thighs where he clung on to him.

"Yeah?"

"Touch me," Nathan groaned.

"I *am* touching you," Wyatt teased, running his hands lightly up and down Nathan's arms.

Nathan swore, grabbed Wyatt's left hand, and tugged it under the water. He placed it firmly on his trembling shaft and shuddered.

"Here. I want you to touch me *here*."

Wyatt obeyed Nathan's tense command and started stroking him in slow, measured movements. He felt Nathan's rising heartbeat echo through to his own chest where they touched and marveled at the delicious feel of Nathan's cock between his fingers.

It wasn't long before Nathan exploded in his hand, his groans of pleasure reverberating against the tiles and his body convulsing beautifully in Wyatt's arms.

Wyatt pressed hot kisses to Nathan's neck and back as Nathan rode his orgasm, his hand moving briskly on his own erection as he rubbed himself toward a climax.

Nathan twisted around and swallowed Wyatt's harsh grunts when he came, his lips demanding as he melded his tongue with Wyatt's, his blue eyes dark with desire where they locked unblinkingly on Wyatt's.

CHAPTER TWENTY-NINE

I'M HAPPY.

Nathan blinked at that sudden thought.

He glanced surreptitiously at the man responsible for the contented feeling coursing through his heart.

Wyatt was engrossed in his work where he sat at his desk opposite Nathan, a faint frown on his handsome face.

Nathan's pulse jumped as he secretly roamed Wyatt's rugged features with his gaze.

God, I'm turning into a hopeless romantic!

Four days had passed since Wyatt's birthday weekend. Though they'd spent every night together since, they hadn't gone all the way again, Wyatt still reluctant to enter Nathan after their first time together.

Though Nathan wouldn't have minded being taken by Wyatt, he knew Wyatt was only thinking about his welfare and the condition of his body. Gay sex was not a territory Nathan was used to treading and he trusted Wyatt's judgement on the matter.

Still, he really wanted to experience the dizzying pleasure of having Wyatt inside him and soon. Nathan pursed his lips as he thought of the weekend ahead.

It was Carter and Elijah's rehearsal dinner on Saturday, with their wedding taking place on Sunday. Nathan had already spotted the paparazzi and the press going around town and questioning the locals about the couple. To Nathan's amusement and delight, the people of Twilight Falls proved to be jealously protective of their star resident and had kept resolutely tight-lipped about his relationship with Elijah.

Carter and Elijah had gotten Finn and Alex's permission to get married at their property; since it was surrounded by acres of private woodland, it would prove a difficult place for the paparazzi to easily infiltrate. Carter's agent had even hired an internationally renowned security firm to oversee the event and the reception that would follow.

Though plenty of news outlets wanted exclusive access to the wedding and had offered eye-watering sums of money for the privilege of being the ones to take pictures of Hollywood's hottest star on his wedding day, Carter had refused all their requests.

This ceremony was one of the many things he wanted only his family and friends to bear witness to.

Though they did not have many relatives between the two of them, Carter and Elijah's friends more than made up the numbers. Nathan had even spotted some big screen names on the guest list that had had him arching his eyebrows.

Nathan cast another look at Wyatt.

Having decided to tell their employees about their relationship when they were good and ready, they'd promised not to do anything risky at work that would expose them until then. Still, Nathan couldn't help the illicit excitement that danced through him at the thought of making out with Wyatt at the office.

"Stop that."

Nathan startled.

Wyatt was staring at him hotly from across the way.

Uh oh. Busted.

"Stop what?" Nathan said innocently.

"Stop looking at me like you want to lick me like a lollipop," Wyatt groaned.

Nathan's cock twitched at the imagery. He swiped his tongue across his lips.

Color stained Wyatt's cheeks. "You're incorrigible, you know that?"

Nathan glanced at the glass wall on his right. It was six o'clock. Everyone bar Adam had left for the day and the receptionist's head was buried deep in a file where he sat with his back to them.

Nathan met Wyatt's gaze again. "I wonder how sturdy your desk is?"

Wyatt's eyes darkened with desire.

"I think we owe it to the manufacturer to find out, don't you?" Nathan rose, crossed the floor to the door, and flicked the switch on the privacy glass. He made his way slowly to Wyatt's desk, his mouth splitting into a grin.

Wyatt sighed as Nathan came around the table. "Don't you have somewhere to be tonight?"

"You mean Dean? He's not coming until later." Nathan maneuvered Wyatt's chair and straddled his lap.

Wyatt groaned when their erections touched.

"You like that?" Nathan rocked his hips slightly.

Wyatt's hands found Nathans butt. "I love everything you do to me."

Butterflies filled Nathan's stomach at his words.

He'd been wanting to confess his feelings to Wyatt for some time now. He took a shaky breath and opened his mouth to say the words he'd been meaning to tell Wyatt.

Wyatt leaned in and took his lips in a scorching kiss.

Nathan's mind went blank. He melted against Wyatt, unable to resist the raw attraction burning between them, his eager tongue meeting Wyatt's invading flesh.

He wasn't sure how long they kissed for.

All Nathan knew was that he didn't want Wyatt to stop kissing him or touching him.

A hungry moan rumbled out of his throat as he sank his fingers into Wyatt's hair and sucked Wyatt's tongue.

A sound registered dimly in the background.

Nathan thought he heard Adam's voice and the door opening.

"Sorry to bother you, but you have a—"

Adam froze mid-sentence and sucked in air.

Wyatt stilled, his widening eyes meeting Nathan's shocked gaze.

"Oh!" Adam blurted out leadenly.

"Nathan?!" someone gasped.

Nathan stiffened. He lifted his mouth off Wyatt's, swallowed, and turned slowly where he still sat on Wyatt's lap.

Dean stood next to a red-faced Adam in the doorway of the office, his expression aghast. Standing a few feet behind them, her trembling hands rising to cover her mouth, her face ashen, was his former fiancée.

Shit.

CHAPTER THIRTY

"Does he have to be here?"

Nathan clenched his jaw at his brother's curt tone.

Wyatt stayed silent where he sat next to Nathan.

"Yes, he does," Nathan replied calmly. "This concerns Wyatt too." His hand found Wyatt's under the table. Wyatt clasped Nathan's fingers and squeezed them reassuringly.

They were in Nathan's kitchen. Dean and Melissa sat opposite them, their faces tense and their coffees untouched.

"I thought you were coming later tonight," Nathan told his brother sedately. His gaze moved briefly to his former fiancée's face. "You didn't tell me you were bringing a guest."

Dean's mouth grew pinched. "It was meant to be a surprise. I—" He paused and raked his hair with hand. "I had something to tell you and I wanted to do it in person." He glanced at Melissa. "*We* wanted to do it in person."

Nathan blinked. Surprise coursed through him as he stared at Dean and Melissa.

Oh. Why didn't I see it before?

"You two are going out."

Dean hesitated before dipping his chin. "We started dating eight months ago." He faltered. "I asked Melissa to marry me last week. She said yes."

Some color returned to Melissa's cheeks. She bit her lip and lowered her eyes to the table. Dean reached over and took her hand.

A fraught silence fell across the room.

Nathan studied the couple opposite him. "Congratulations."

Dean blinked. Melissa lifted her head and stared at Nathan.

"Did you think I would be upset?" Nathan said quietly.

The haunted look in Melissa's eyes made him feel like a cad all over again.

"I'm the one who practically abandoned you at the altar, Mel. You don't need my permission to date Dean." Nathan smiled lopsidedly. "Although, truth be told, I'm not quite sure what you see in him. He's a handful."

"Hey!" Dean protested.

Melissa's mouth twitched slightly.

The tension inside the room started to fade a little.

Melissa looked at Wyatt before gazing at Nathan once more.

"Since when have you been—" She stopped, as if she couldn't complete the sentence.

Nathan noted the trace of bitterness in her voice and swallowed a sigh.

I can't say I blame her.

"Gay?" Nathan shrugged. "I'm not."

Dean's eyes widened. "Then why were you kissing that guy?!"

Wyatt stiffened at the other man's accusing tone.

Nathan narrowed his eyes at his brother. "I would appreciate it if you did not insult my boyfriend under my own roof."

Dean opened and closed his mouth soundlessly.

"You make it sound as if you two are in a relationship!" he finally spat out.

"We are."

Dean drew a sharp breath at Nathan's statement. Melissa's fingers twitched where she held Dean's hand.

"And he has a name," Nathan added coolly. "It's Wyatt Batista."

Dean glared at Wyatt. "Did you seduce my brother?!"

A muscle danced in Wyatt's jawline. "Seeing as you're Nathan's family, I'm going to pretend you didn't just ask me that question."

Nathan's stomach twisted at the smoldering anger he could feel radiating off Wyatt. He knew Wyatt was more upset about the fact that Dean was attacking his own brother than anything else.

Dean's hot gaze switched to Nathan.

"Do you have any idea what this will do to Mom and Dad? They'll be devastated!"

"You don't know that," Nathan retorted.

"Oh come on!" Dean snapped. "They still go to church every Sunday. You know how old-fashioned they are in their views!"

Nathan clenched his jaw.

It wasn't as if he'd buried his head in the sand when he'd decided to pursue Wyatt. He'd known the day would come when he may have to tell his parents that he was in a relationship with a man and that the chances they would reject him and Wyatt were high.

Still, none of that had deterred Nathan.

And it still doesn't.

He turned to Wyatt. "Would you mind going home for the night? This is going to take a while."

Guilt knotted Nathan's belly when he saw the hurt that flashed in Wyatt's eyes. He rose and guided Wyatt into the hall.

"Are you sure you want me to go?" Wyatt muttered.

Nathan clasped Wyatt's face and pressed a sweet kiss to his mouth.

"I know you think I'm rejecting you right now," he mumbled against Wyatt's lips. "I'm not. They're never gonna see sense if you're in the room. I need to convince them my way."

Wyatt hesitated. "Okay."

Nathan's heart twisted as he watched Wyatt walk down the path and climb inside his SUV. He knew Wyatt was still doubtful about what he'd just said. He watched the vehicle's taillights until they disappeared down the road, closed the door, and headed back inside the house.

Nathan was determined to show his family how

wonderful Wyatt was. Just as he was determined to demonstrate to Wyatt that he intended to spend the rest of his life with him.

❧

IZZY LOOKED UP FROM THE TV WHEN SHE HEARD THE front door open. She glanced at the clock on the wall with frown.

He's early.

Wyatt ambled into the room a moment later and sat down heavily on the couch beside her.

Unease stirred inside Izzy at his leaden expression.

Wyatt dropped his head back, closed his eyes, and sighed heavily.

"What's wrong?" Izzy murmured.

"Nathan's brother and former fiancée showed up expectedly at the office tonight." He rubbed a hand down his face. "They caught us kissing."

Izzy inhaled sharply. "Uh oh."

A wry grimace twisted Wyatt's lips. "That's an understatement."

Izzy switched the TV off and sat cross-legged on the couch.

"What happened?"

"We went to Nathan's place to talk. Things started to get ugly, so Nathan asked me to leave."

Izzy narrowed her eyes slightly at her brother's defeatist tone.

"Why do you sound as if you thought that was a bad thing?"

Wyatt groaned. "Oh, come on! It's obvious, isn't it? I mean, he's hardly going to choose me over his family."

Izzy's frown turned into a full-blown scowl.

"What?" Wyatt said defensively.

"Since when are you such a coward?"

Wyatt's jaw dropped at Izzy's accusation.

"What?!" he spluttered after a speechless moment.

"I'm saying you're acting like a coward right now, Wyatt," Izzy said sharply. "You're so damn scared that Nathan went out with you on a whim, you're looking for any excuse to break things off with him and give him a way out."

Wyatt paled.

Remorse stabbed through Izzy at his haunted expression. She gritted her teeth.

This is for his own damn good!

"I know you won't like me saying this, but if you keep shying away from taking a risk like you did with Brandon, you will live to regret it, Wyatt," Izzy said hotly. "Nathan is the one for you. Don't let him slip so easily through your fingers."

"She's beautiful," Wyatt mumbled.

Izzy blinked, confused. "What?"

"The woman Nathan was going to marry." Wyatt swallowed convulsively. "She's beautiful. What's to say —what's to say it won't happen again? That he won't fall in love with another woman? That he won't want kids of his own in the future? And the last thing I want is for Nathan to have a fallout with his family because of me!"

Emotion clogged Izzy's throat at Wyatt's shaky voice. She leaned over and hugged him tightly.

"Is that what you've been thinking all this time?!" she whispered tremulously.

Wyatt hesitated before nodding. He pressed his hot face in the crook of her neck.

A stilted silence fell across the room.

"Nathan is serious about you, Wyatt," Izzy finally said. "He's not the kind of guy who would enter a relationship with a man on a wild impulse. He must have given this a lot of thought over the last month. So, trust him." She pulled back and pressed a kiss to her brother's forehead. "Trust Nathan, Wyatt."

Wyatt faltered before dipping his chin. He headed upstairs to his bedroom a short while later, his expression still sad.

Izzy chewed her lip where she sat staring into space.

Her cell phone buzzed on the coffee table.

Izzy nearly did a double take when she saw the caller ID.

It was Nathan.

"Hey, how are you holding up?" Izzy said into the speaker.

Nathan hesitated. "Did Wyatt tell you what happened?"

"Yeah." Izzy sighed. "He looked pretty miserable when he came home."

"Shit," Nathan mumbled.

"You okay?"

Nathan's voice turned wry. "Never better. My

brother hates me and my former fiancée thinks I'm a douchebag."

Izzy smiled. "It could be worse."

"How?"

"There could be cooties. Or snakes."

Nathan laughed at that.

Izzy grinned. "I take it from your tone that you're still dead set on making an honest man out of my brother?"

"That's why I called. I need your help."

CHAPTER THIRTY-ONE

"This is a bit like déja vu."

Wyatt glanced at his sister where she stood twirling a champagne flute next to him.

Carter and Elijah were taking pictures under the pretty pergola wreathed with scarlet roses and white camellias that had been erected on the edge of the forest surrounding Finn and Alex's home. Maisie looked resplendent in a cream taffeta and lace dress where she stood between the two grooms, her face flushed and beaming with happiness.

It was Carter and Elijah's wedding day and it had gone as beautifully as Wyatt had expected it would. The love the two men shared almost had the air glowing when they'd exchanged their vows in the fairy tale woodland clearing where the ceremony had taken place a short while ago, and there hadn't been a dry eye in the house by the time they'd shared their first official kiss as a married couple. Even the stoic Izzy had sniffled and sobbed her way through the ritual.

Wyatt scanned the crowd with his gaze.

Carter and Elijah's guests milled through two large white marquees set in the grounds. Although Finn and Alex had offered to open up their home for the reception, Carter and Elijah had refused and insisted they couldn't impose on them after everything he and Alex had done for them.

Where is he?

The frustration that had been gnawing at Wyatt for the last three days had his stomach practically in knots. Although he and Nathan had seen each other at the rehearsal dinner yesterday, Nathan had been strangely evasive and had disappeared before they could have a proper talk.

All Wyatt knew was that Dean and Melissa had gone back to Seattle on Friday after spending the day with Nathan. He'd half expected Nathan to call him over afterward but that hadn't happened either.

Is he having doubts about our relationship?

Wyatt shook his head slightly to dispel his negative thoughts.

Izzy's right. I can't just give up without a fight.

Determination filled Wyatt.

Nathan isn't Brandon.

"That's some frown," Izzy drawled.

Wyatt clenched his jaw. "Have you seen Nathan?"

Something flashed in Izzy's eyes. "I think I saw him go for a walk in the woods earlier."

Wyatt stared at her suspiciously before gazing in the direction of the dense woodland crowding Finn and Alex's property. "It's dark."

Izzy shrugged. "He had a flashlight."

Wyatt hesitated before handing his champagne flute to his sister and heading for the trees, her amused gaze following him.

Ten minutes later and Wyatt still hadn't found any sign of Nathan.

He was headed back to the reception when he heard rustling to his left. The beam of his cell phone flashlight washed across greenery as he aimed it in that direction.

"Oh. I'm sorry!" he mumbled.

Wyatt lowered the phone hastily and hurried back toward the marquee lights.

That was Drake, right? Who was the other guy?

All Wyatt had glimpsed of the man whose body had been entwined with Drake's was a tattoo running up the side of his neck and a silver earring glinting at his earlobe.

Izzy was waiting for him when he came out of the cover of the trees.

"I found Nathan. He's waiting for you on Finn and Alex's terrace."

Wyatt stilled when he saw his sister's guarded expression.

"What's going on?"

Izzy smiled. "It's not what you think. Just go."

Wyatt's heart started pounding as he headed toward Finn and Alex's house.

He bumped into a few guests who'd gone to use the facilities and was swallowed by shadows when he entered the open plan lounge that led to the rear of the property.

Wyatt slowed when he saw the fairy lights strung across the deck.

They hadn't been there the last time he'd looked. Nor had the small, white canopy that had been erected on the edge of the terrace, where it looked over the creek.

Wyatt's pulse accelerated when he stepped outside and saw the man waiting under the awning.

Nathan looked breathtakingly handsome in his tuxedo where he stood bathed under the soft lights, his expression somewhat nervous.

"Hey," he said softly.

Wyatt slowly closed the distance between them, his steps hesitant. His eyes widened when he clocked the champagne bottle and ice bucket behind Nathan.

Hope filled Wyatt as he met the blue eyes locked on him. Wild, crazy hope. It rushed through his heart and soul, obliterating any doubt he'd ever had about the man he had fallen in love with.

"What's going on?" Wyatt breathed.

Nathan flashed him a dazzling smile. He waited until Wyatt joined him before taking Wyatt's left hand in his own.

"I know I've worried you these past few days. And for that, I'm sorry." His eyes darkened with emotion as he gazed at Wyatt. "There's something I've been meaning to tell you. And something I want to ask you."

Nathan took a shaky breath before taking a small,

blue velvet box out of his pocket. He dropped down on one knee in front of Wyatt.

Wyatt froze.

This—this isn't happening! I'm dreaming this right now!

A gasp rose behind him.

He looked over his shoulder and saw Izzy, Tristan, Hunter, Drake, Alex, and Finn standing near the door to the terrace, smiles on their faces. Carter and Elijah appeared behind them, somewhat breathless, as if they'd ran all the way there.

"Did we miss it?!" Elijah panted.

"Nope." Izzy grinned, her eyes swimming with tears as she met Wyatt's stunned gaze. "He's just getting to the good part." She looked at the man kneeling before Wyatt.

Wyatt stared at Nathan, his mouth dry and his heart pounding so hard he thought he'd faint.

"Do you know how I managed to convince Dean and Melissa that you were the only one for me?"

Wyatt swallowed and shook his head.

"I told them that this wasn't about gender," Nathan said, his eyes glittering like jewels. "That I have never had a romantic interest in men. That I still don't." His fingers clenched around Wyatt's. "I told them that you just crept into my heart, slowly but surely. With every smile. With every conversation we had. Every time we went out as friends. Every time you invited me into your life and home. You seeped into my senses and my soul, as certain as the moon and the tides. And I told them that, one day, I woke up and all I could see was you. The one I had fallen in love with. The person I want to spend the rest of my life with."

A sob left Izzy. Elijah sniffed and wiped at his eyes.

Wyatt's vision swam with unshed tears as he gazed at the man before him.

Nathan removed a beautiful silver band from the jewelry box.

"I love you, Wyatt Batista. You make me happy in ways I never imagined I could be happy. You complete me. Will you—"

Nathan gasped when Wyatt hauled him to his feet and took his mouth in a blistering kiss.

"Yes," Wyatt mumbled hoarsely. "A thousand times, yes."

Nathan's hands trembled as he slipped the band on Wyatt's left ring finger. Air whooshed out of him when Wyatt suddenly crouched and lifted him over his shoulder, fireman style. Wyatt turned and stormed across the terrace, his arms hooked securely around Nathan's body.

"Izzy?"

"Yeah?"

"Don't come home tonight," Wyatt growled.

Nathan groaned and buried his flushed face in his hands while their friends chuckled.

"You animal!" Izzy laughed.

CHAPTER THIRTY-TWO

By the time they entered Wyatt's home, Nathan was so hard he thought he'd explode at the first touch of Wyatt's hands.

Wyatt's movements had been sure and steady as he negotiated the mountain roads and the town streets on their drive back. Nathan always felt safe when Wyatt was at the wheel. Yet, tonight, he'd wished he'd driven just that much faster.

Wyatt locked the front door and grabbed Nathan's hand. He led him up the stairs, his skin scalding where his palm touched Nathan's.

"Say something," Nathan mumbled.

"I love you."

Nathan's heart swelled with joy.

"I'm going to make love to you so hard you'll see stars."

Nathan's ass contracted at Wyatt's hotly murmured words.

"Then I'll do it again and again, until neither of us can catch our breath."

"Oh God," Nathan mumbled.

Wyatt flicked on the lamps scattered around his bedroom and pulled Nathan into his arms. He angled his head and kissed him hard and deep. By the time Wyatt lifted his mouth from Nathan's, Nathan's mind was a puddle of goo.

Wyatt undressed Nathan hastily and pushed him on the bed.

Nathan's breaths shuddered out of him as he watched Wyatt undo his own neck tie and the buttons of his dress shirt, his large hands moving deftly.

"Wait."

Wyatt paused and looked at him, puzzled.

Nathan scooted over to the edge of the bed, grabbed his trousers off the floor, and removed something from a pocket.

Wyatt stared at the red silk scarf in his hand.

"Is that—"

"Yeah." Nathan grinned, lay on his back, and carefully tied the scarf around the base of his erection. He finished off the adornment with a pretty bow and folded his hands behind his head.

"This is one of my fantasies. You stripping out a tux while I'm naked and wearing this."

"Fuck!" Wyatt mumbled.

"Do it slowly," Nathan commanded. He lifted his left foot and kneaded Wyatt's straining erection teasingly with his toes. "I want to savor my gift."

Wyatt's flushed cheeks and dilated pupils told Nathan exactly what he thought of this. He took his sweet time stripping out of his clothes, every inch of toned skin and bulging muscle he exposed heightening Nathan's arousal.

Nathan reached down and started stroking himself when Wyatt pulled the zipper over his swollen dick. He licked his lips as Wyatt kicked off his pants and hooked his fingers into the elastic band of his black boxers. Wyatt pushed the material down inch by inch. His erection finally sprang free, thick and hard and shiny.

Nathan's belly contracted painfully.

I want him in my mouth. Now!

He moved onto his knees, yanked Wyatt close, and went down on him.

Wyatt hissed as Nathan clasped his shaft and licked him from the root all the way to the glistening tip. He cradled Nathan's chin in one hand and guided his cock to Nathan's lips.

Nathan looked up at Wyatt from under his lashes, opened his mouth, and took him inside.

"Ah!" Wyatt dropped his head back, his eyes closing and a rictus of pleasure distorting his features. He looked down again and met Nathan's heated gaze as Nathan started blowing him.

Nathan continued rubbing himself while he relished Wyatt's thick rod. It filled his cheeks and rubbed along his tongue, hot and silky and full of Wyatt's musky scent and taste. He couldn't believe how much he enjoyed doing this to Wyatt or how powerful he felt when he brought Wyatt to an earth-shattering climax with just his lips and tongue.

Wyatt widened his stance, clasped Nathan's head with none too gentle hands, and started thrusting his hips, guttural groans and grunts of pleasure tumbling from his lips as he gave in to his instincts to fuck and to possess.

Nathan's hand accelerated on his own cock, his fingers squeezing and rubbing his inflamed flesh harder and faster, his impending orgasm sending electricity sparking along his nerve endings. He came seconds before Wyatt exploded at the back of his throat, their sounds of pleasure echoing harshly around the room.

Wyatt pulled his spent cock out of Nathan's mouth a moment later and followed him down onto the bed. They lay panting for precious minutes, bodies pressed together and hands intertwined.

Wyatt finally lifted his head and kissed Nathan all over again, his eyes blazing green with passion. He worked his way slowly down Nathan's body with his fingers, lips, and tongue, every gasp, every hiss, every groan Nathan made fuel to the fire burning between them. By the time he reached the scarf tied around Nathan's cock, Nathan was a hot, moaning mess.

"*Wyatt*," Nathan mumbled in a tortured voice, sweat beading his face and chest, his swollen, wet nipples still tingling from Wyatt's ardent ministrations.

"Yes, Nathan?" Wyatt's breath washed teasingly across Nathan's fresh erection where he lay between Nathan's bent legs. He pressed hot kisses to the insides of Nathan's thighs, teeth nipping and delivering tender love bites on his quivering flesh.

"Take me!" Nathan begged.

"I'm gonna need you to elaborate on that."

Nathan reached down and grasped his swollen cock.

"Fuck me with your mouth. Suck me, Wyatt!"

A harsh cry left Nathan as Wyatt finally obliged his command. He twisted his hands in the pillow under his head and surrendered his body to Wyatt, his hips dancing off the bed and driving his straining cock in and out of Wyatt's hungry mouth.

He was nearing his orgasm when Wyatt suddenly pulled off him, tightened the scarf at the base of his dick, and started stroking his thighs and belly with featherlight touches.

"Wyatt?!" Nathan panted.

"Sssh," Wyatt hushed.

Wyatt gently rubbed and kissed his cock again. It took a minute for Nathan to realize that Wyatt was edging him. Nathan groaned and gasped as Wyatt brought him close to a climax then withdrew, causing his body to shudder and writhe in a constant flux of ever-growing pleasure as minutes went by.

"*Oh!*"

White light throbbed across Nathan's vision when his belly suddenly clenched violently and his cock pulsed. To his shock, his erection remained at full mast and he failed to ejaculate.

"Was that—?"

CHAPTER THIRTY-THREE

"A dry orgasm?" Wyatt pressed sweet kisses to Nathan's twitching belly, his own cock painfully stiff where it rubbed against the bedsheet. "Yup, it was."

By the time Nathan really came, Wyatt had tortured his sensitive body to two more dry climaxes. Nathan's hoarse shout bounced off the bedroom walls as he exploded with a fierceness that drove his cum deep inside Wyatt's eager throat, his hips jerking and dancing erratically in Wyatt's firm grip, his straining nipples hard and rosy pink as he arched his back.

Wyatt gulped and swallowed it all, eager to taste everything Nathan had to give him.

Nathan was still shivering and shuddering from the ecstasy he had just experienced when Wyatt removed the scarf around his spent cock, propped a couple of pillows next to him, and rolled him onto his belly. Wyatt fought down his base impulse as he gazed at Nathan's trembling body.

All he wanted to do was shove his thick cock deep inside Nathan's ass and ride him until the morning.

He clenched his jaw.

Slow down. This is still new for him.

Wyatt carefully parted Nathan's cleft with his hands and exposed his enticing entrance.

Nathan's pink pucker contracted prettily under Wyatt's hungry stare. A low hum left Nathan's lips. He angled his hips higher, seeking whatever it was Wyatt wanted to do to him.

Wyatt cursed at the seductive move. He pulled away just long enough to grab condoms and lube from the nightstand drawer, spread Nathan's opening with his thumbs, and flicked and circled his furrowed tongue all around the tight folds guarding Nathan's back passage.

Wyatt might as well have let off a bomb from the way Nathan reacted. He soon lost track of time as he prepared Nathan's body for his cock, Nathan's lusty keens and moans filling his ears.

Wyatt hissed when he finally pushed a finger inside Nathan.

Shit. He's so fucking tight.

He swore when Nathan squeezed his finger and looked at him sultrily over his shoulder.

"More," Nathan breathed, lips swollen and red from Wyatt's kisses, and cheeks and chest flushed with desire.

Wyatt carefully thrust his finger in and out of Nathan's body before pouring lube all over his twitching folds and pushing a second finger in. They both groaned when he reached the ring of inner muscles guarding Nathan's passage.

Wyatt scissored his fingers and kissed and nipped at Nathan's butt cheeks while he sought the soft bump of his prostate. Nathan's guttural cry told him when he'd found his sweet spot.

He slipped a third finger inside Nathan and worked him open, Nathan's passage clenching and spasming around him.

"Now!" Nathan moaned a while later. "Enter me, Wyatt!"

Blood pounded in Wyatt's chest and cock as he sheathed his rock-hard rod and brought the swollen tip to Nathan's entrance. They both hissed when he pushed inside in a slow, deep thrust, only stopping when he was seated to the hilt, his pubes and balls kissing Nathan's butt cheeks.

Nathan reached back and gripped Wyatt's left hip, his fingers biting into his flesh and urging him on.

Wyatt leaned forward, twisted a hand in Nathan's hair, and pulled his head back until his spine arced beautifully and he was panting with anticipation.

Wyatt pulled his slick cock out until only the tip sat inside Nathan's hole and pushed back inside with a deep rolling motion.

"Ah!"

The way Nathan moaned and convulsed sweetly on the bed told Wyatt he'd just climaxed. He carried on thrusting in and out of Nathan's body, his breaths leaving his throat in harsh gasps and grunts, his cock tingling as it was squeezed lovingly by Nathan's passage.

The room faded around Wyatt. Time stilled.

All that was left were their bodies mating sensuously, giving and receiving in equal measure, the bed rocking gently and the springs squeaking beneath them while their hearts pounded in tandem and their breathless sounds of pleasure echoed in their ears.

By the time Wyatt came, he'd brought Nathan to another splendid orgasm.

He waited until they'd both stopped convulsing before pulling out of Nathan. He disposed of the used condom and yanked Nathan up onto his knees.

Nathan's head lolled onto Wyatt's shoulder as Wyatt guided his legs around his waist.

Wyatt tipped Nathan's chin up where he straddled his lap and kissed him sweetly, his breathing still ragged.

"I don't think I can move," Nathan mumbled.

Wyatt smiled and nuzzled their noses together. "We're just getting started."

"Izzy was right," Nathan protested weakly. "You're an animal."

Wyatt chuckled, his heart swelling with affection. He rained kisses all over Nathan's face and stroked Nathan's back and thighs lightly with his hands. It wasn't long before Nathan was sporting a fresh erection and was rearing to go once more, his blue eyes dark with lust and his body shuddering with anticipation.

Wyatt waited until Nathan was begging him to take him before reaching for a condom.

Nathan grabbed his hand. "Wait."

Wyatt stilled and gave him a puzzled look.

Nathan bit his lip. "Have you ever taken anyone bareback before?"

Wyatt's eyes widened and his cock throbbed where it was cradled by Nathan's groin.

"No."

"Thank God," Nathan mumbled.

"Is that really something to be thankful about?" Wyatt groaned.

"It is." Color stained Nathan's cheeks as he stared into Wyatt's eyes. "It'll be a first for both of us."

Wyatt stiffened. "You don't seriously want to—"

"I do." Nathan kissed Wyatt and nipped at his lower lip with his strong, white teeth. "And I am. Deathly serious. I want to feel you."

Wyatt shuddered as Nathan trailed his knuckles on his bare erection.

"All of you," Nathan breathed.

Wyatt cursed, his fingers biting into Nathan's hips.

"Please," Nathan pleaded softly against his lips.

"That's not fair," Wyatt mumbled. "You know I can't refuse you when you beg me like that."

"Then do it." Nathan grabbed on to Wyatt's shoulders, pressed his feet on the bed, and rose above Wyatt's groin.

Wyatt swore as Nathan guided the tip of his dick to his hole.

"Fill me up, Wyatt. Come inside me."

Wyatt gnashed his teeth, coated his cock liberally with lube, spread Nathan open with his hands, and pushed up slowly.

How he didn't explode at his first bareback penetration, he didn't know.

All Wyatt could do was feel.

The heat and sweet softness of Nathan's passage as it steadily swallowed him whole. The tight muscles lovingly squeezing his steely shaft as they adjusted to the penetration. Nathan's heartbeat pounding against his chest. Nathan's arms wrapping tightly around his shoulders and neck as Wyatt set the rhythm of their lovemaking, hips pumping and driving his dick in and out of Nathan's hole. Nathan's gasps and moans and cries.

This wasn't just sex or a mating of bodies.

This was Nathan and him fusing their hearts and souls together.

This was love and acceptance and a promise for their future.

Nathan's cock rubbed slickly against Wyatt's belly as he danced and writhed on Wyatt's cock, his mouth open on harsh sounds of pleasure and his passage contracting rhythmically around the thick intruder impaling him.

He stiffened in Wyatt's arms when he neared his climax, his cries growing more lustful while his ass clamped tighter and tighter around Wyatt's throbbing cock.

He came seconds before Wyatt, his body bowing

and his ass spasming with sweet violence on Wyatt's shaft while his dick exploded hot cum all over their chests.

Wyatt closed his teeth on Nathan's left shoulder as his own orgasm bore down on him, his belly tightening with a growing knot of tension and his hips pumping fitfully off the bed, the frame squeaking and groaning beneath their bodies. A dizzying ringing filled his ears as the first wave of his orgasm pulsed through his cock.

A feral grunt ripped from Wyatt's throat as he ejaculated, the pleasure drowning his body so intense it was almost pain. His dick jerked and twitched and swelled as he emptied his thick, hot seed inside Nathan's body, the waves of ecstasy seemingly never-ending.

It was some time before awareness returned. With it came Nathan's tender kiss as their bodies trembled and shuddered against one another. Wyatt bit his lip.

Nathan's passage was hot and snug and wet with his cum where he still cradled Wyatt's cock.

Wyatt made to pull out and groaned when Nathan clamped down on him.

"Just a bit longer," Nathan begged softly, his face pressed against Wyatt's shoulder.

Wyatt wrapped his arms tightly around the man in his arms.

There was no way he could deny Nathan his sweet request.

"Was that good for you too?"

A low chuckle left Nathan. "Seeing as I almost

passed out again, the answer to that question is a resounding yes."

Wyatt swallowed a curse when Nathan's laughter caused his hole to squeeze his dick.

"We need to clean you up."

"In a minute."

Wyatt sighed. "Seriously, the sooner we get my cum out of you, the better it'll be for you. Let me take you to the shower."

Nathan lifted his head and narrowed his eyes at Wyatt.

"Alright. But you have to promise me something."

Wyatt studied him warily. "What?"

A sinful smile curved Nathan's lips. He brought his mouth to Wyatt's right ear and nipped at his lobe with his teeth.

"Promise that you'll fill me up again and again before morning comes."

Nathan's smile turned into full blown laughter when Wyatt swore, shuffled off the bed, and carried him buck naked into the bathroom, his cock still wedged firmly inside Nathan's ass.

THE END

Can reformed bad boy Drake Jackson tame a wild rockstar?
Get Drake (Twilight Falls 5)

Have you read the Nights series yet? Find out if Gabe
Anderson accepts Cam Sorvino's promise of one night
of mindless pleasure to help him overcome his phobia
of intimacy!
Get One Night (Nights 1)
Turn the page to read an extract now!

ONE NIGHT (NIGHTS #1) SPECIAL PREVIEW

CHAPTER ONE

*W*HAT THE HELL AM *I* DOING HERE?

Gabe Anderson scanned the crowded club in the mirror opposite the bar before looking down into his scotch with a self-deprecating smile. This had seemed like such a great idea an hour ago, when he'd been staring at an empty weekend in an even emptier apartment.

Saron was located in a side alley, a short walk from Shinjuku's main club strip. Despite its somewhat shady location, the place oozed style.

Gabe had hesitated when he'd seen the suited doorman guarding the entrance and wondered if access was by invitation only. He only knew of *Saron* from overhearing his clients mention it a few nights ago. From what he'd made of their excited conversation, it was *the* place to hang out in Shinjuku if you were of a particular sexual inclination.

The doorman had checked Gabe over for all of three seconds before wordlessly unclipping the rope from the stanchions framing the steel doors. He had obviously passed some kind of test, though what it was he didn't know.

Beyond a foyer with a cloakroom manned by a male attendant who looked like he'd walked straight out of a *GQ* shoot were a set of shallow steps leading to a wide, sunken floor.

Despite the butterflies churning his stomach, Gabe had stopped and stared appreciatively at the decor. As a consultant for one of Chicago's biggest design firms, he could tell how much money had gone into giving *Saron* its unique look. The club was drowned in deep reds, dark purples, and rich earth tones. Scattered across the oak floor were Brazilian cherry wood tables and armchairs boasting plush velvet upholstery and satin cushions. Discrete booths dotted the walls and afforded privacy to those who needed it, although the muted lighting provided enough of that as it was. A polished mahogany counter with wine-red leather and walnut stools ran the length of the bar on the right.

At the far end of the room, a woman in a black cocktail dress stood on a raised podium. She was crooning a song in a sultry, deep voice, her eyes closed and her glossy ruby lips glistening in the mellow spotlight. Behind her, cymbals vibrated gently, a piano tinkled, and a saxophone hummed, the sounds somehow rising above the voices of the men packing the place.

It was as he'd made his way to the bar that Gabe had realized why the doorman had let him in. From the looks of the club's patrons, *Saron* catered exclusively to an upscale clientele. He was willing to bet a week's wages none of the suits in the place cost less than five hundred dollars.

"Ah, fresh meat."

Gabe froze in the act of sitting on a barstool, his gaze swinging up to meet a pair of amused green eyes on the other side of the mahogany counter.

"Excuse me?" he said stiffly.

The bartender, a striking blond in a slate, silk tuxedo vest and crisp white shirt, flashed him a grin.

"I've not seen you around these parts before. What will it be?"

Gabe swallowed, wondering whether the man had seen straight through him and grasped the reason he had come to *Saron*.

"What will what be?" he mumbled, unable to mask the apprehension in his voice.

The bartender pursed his lips and observed him with a shrewd expression before leaning across the counter.

"Relax," he murmured in Gabe's left ear. "I can tell it's your first time in a place like this. If you keep up that deer-in-the-headlights look you've got painted across that pretty face of yours, you're gonna be a target for every sleaze ball in this club. And, trust me, they might be wearing thousand-dollar ensembles, but some of these assholes are nothing but dirty pigs in suits."

An involuntary bark of laughter left Gabe's lips at the mental image the bartender's words had conjured. The sound carried along the counter, drawing stares.

The knot of tension that had been sitting between Gabe's shoulder blades ever since he ventured into Shinjuku eased as he smiled at the bartender.

"I've never been called pretty before."

The guy winked.

"Trust me, you're the hottest thing on legs in this place right now. Besides me, of course."

Gabe chuckled and ordered a scotch, his confidence boosted by the compliment.

Two months had passed since he'd relocated to Tokyo from Chicago. When his bosses had sprung the offer on Gabe in early spring, the chance of a fresh start in a place void of the dark memories that had plagued him for eight years was too much of an attractive proposition for him to reject. He'd left Chicago with two suitcases and five crates full of books and artwork, the only things he had to show after a decade in the city.

Though he had been prepared for the culture shock, life in Tokyo had still come as a surprise, albeit an invigorating one. He had always had an interest in the country and its intoxicating mix of traditional and contemporary customs ever since he made his first business trip to the Japanese branch of the firm four years ago.

Luckily, his new position suited him to a T. He had thrown himself into his first assignment with his usual drive and passion, leading the team under him to make good on a project, one which his predecessor had only made a half-assed attempt to complete. He had delivered on time, on budget, and on schedule, despite the nearly impossible deadline. The crazy hours and weekends he had put in had not gone unnoticed, and the praise lavished on his team at the grand opening of their client's luxury hotel earlier that week was all the acknowledgment Gabe needed to realize he had made the right choice in moving to this city. The fact that the money he was making could easily afford him a two-bedroom condo in the exclusive neighborhood of Meguro didn't hurt, either.

Yet, despite having relocated thousands of miles to the other side of the world, his mind would not let go of the bite of his past. Which was why, when faced with the prospect of his first free weekend and the boxes he had yet to unpack, he had looked up *Saron*'s location on the spur of the moment and decided to take a gamble.

He had promised himself this move would not be just a fresh start for his mind, but for his body, too. That he would start taking risks in his personal life again. That he would not let the bastard who had made it impossible for him to ever have a satisfying physical relationship win.

Fifteen minutes into his first drink and Gabe wondered whether he had made a bad choice. So far, Ethan, the bartender, had helped him field a burly, yakuza-looking type with tattoos up the side of his neck, three old men with sweaty palms and bald patches, and a couple of young guys who looked barely past the legal age of drinking.

With his lean build, dark hair, and blue eyes, Gabe knew he was an attractive prospect. Add in that he was a foreigner and he was coming to the conclusion that he had become a beeline for all the men in the bar who wanted to make a conquest out of the white guy – a white notch in the proverbial bedpost. They all wanted to fuck him or be fucked by him.

A cynical half-smile twisted his lips at that thought. If only they knew.

He raised a hand to the back of his neck and rubbed the warm spot that had been bothering him for a while. Something made him look up from his drink then – call it instinct or that subconscious voice that warns of imminent danger. Movement in the mirror opposite the bar caught his gaze. Or, more precisely, a lack of it.

Stormy gray eyes pierced him from the other end of the club. They locked on him, a beam of light in the gloom. Transfixing him. Immobilizing him.

Gabe's breath caught in his throat, every muscle in his body tightening in fight-or-flight mode.

The man sat apart from the crowd, alone at a table that could have accommodated three, a tumbler full of dark liquid clasped casually in his left hand. His red silk tie was crooked, as if he had slipped a finger through the knot to loosen it. The top two buttons on his white shirt were open, revealing tan skin covering toned muscles and a hint of curls.

Gabe couldn't tell whether his hair was dark brown or dirty blond. It was hard to say in the dim light. What wasn't hard to see were the subtle and not-so-subtle stares the other men in the bar were giving the stranger.

With his stubbled face, smoldering looks, and what appeared to be an incredibly ripped body beneath a custom-tailored charcoal suit, the man looked like a king sitting on a throne, commanding a roomful of servants. Servants who appeared more than willing to either get fucked by him or fuck him if he so much as lifted his little finger.

And a man like that would not have to ask twice.

Envy and irritation flashed through Gabe at that thought, shattering the spell he found himself under. He broke eye contact, shocked by the feelings suddenly flooding him, and glared at his half-empty glass. It seemed to mock him, as if it were a reflection of his own life. A half-empty, broken shell. Incapable of touching someone or to be touched.

Gabe lifted the glass and downed the rest of the drink with an angry flick of his wrist. Fire singed his throat. He welcomed the burning sensation, hoping it would calm the pounding in his chest and the tightness in his belly and groin that told him his body had reacted to the stranger.

A full glass of scotch appeared next to his empty tumbler.

Gabe looked up at Ethan, puzzled.

A remorseful grimace flashed across the bartender's face. "Looks like we're no longer the two hottest bastards in this joint. Here, compliments of the King."

Gabe stared at the drink before slowly looking over his shoulder, his pulse picking up speed.

Gray Eyes raised his glass in a toast. A teasing smile played on his sculptured lips before he knocked back his drink.

You're kidding me.

Gabe tried to block out the heated tingle running across his skin at the stranger's cocky smirk and the way his powerful throat muscles worked when he swallowed. He turned to Ethan.

"That's his *actual* name?"

Ethan grunted. "Well, no. But the asshole sure acts like one."

There was movement in the mirror opposite Gabe.

Read One Night today

AFTERWORD

To all my friends who helped make this possible. You know who you are.

To you, my readers. Thank you for reading Wyatt and Nathan's story. I hope you loved the fourth book in the Twilight Falls series. I would be grateful if you could leave a review on Goodreads or on the store where you purchased this book. Reviews help readers like you find my books and I truly appreciate your honest opinions about my stories.

Make sure to sign up to my store newsletter for special deals on my books and new release alerts. Or you can sign up to my author newsletter instead to get upcoming release notifications, sneak peeks, and giveaways.

BOOKS BY A.M. SALINGER

NIGHTS

One Night - 1

The Escort - 2

Tokyo Heat - 3

Sweet Obsession - 4

Sweet Possession - 5

The Proposition - 6

Undisclosed - 7

Hush - 8

One Day - 9

TWILIGHT FALLS

Alex - 1

Carter - 2

Hunter - 3

Wyatt - 4

Drake - 5

Tristan - 6

Miles - 7

ABOUT THE AUTHOR

Ava Marie Salinger is the romance pen name of an Amazon bestselling author with a passion for writing addictive tales. Known for her action-packed and thrilling urban fantasy novels, she has expanded her repertoire with the introduction of the M/M urban fantasy romance series Fallen Messengers. Additionally, she has penned the scorching hot contemporary M/M romance series Nights and Twilight Falls as A.M. Salinger. When not immersed in her writing, Ava can be found curating inspiring music playlists, indulging in her love for nature, marveling at the latest gadgets, and savoring Chinese cuisine.

You can find all of Ava's books on her author store at shop.adstarrling.com